THE LEGACIES OF BRIGADIER STATION

SARAH WILLIAMS

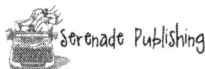

Serenade Publishing

Cover design: Lana Pecherczyk.

The Legacies of Brigadier Station / Sarah Williams. – 1st ed. AUS English.

Serenade Publishing
www.serenadepublishing.com

SARAH WILLIAMS

LOVE STORIES THAT WILL ROPE YOU IN

To my daughters, Raphaella and Arabella

CHAPTER 1

*L*achlan McGuire had been sober for ten months and twenty-two days.

It had been a struggle and like his AA sponsor, Michael, had said, "You have to make the decision not to drink, every day."

He let his fingers touch the gold aluminium of the beer can. The good samaritan who had supplied the esky of drinks clearly hadn't known that putting soft drinks in the same ice-filled esky as the wine, beer, and pre-mixes would cause Lachie such despair.

It would be so easy for him to pull out that can of sweet amber, slide it into a cooler so nobody would know, and give in to the urge. The urge he had supressed for such a long time. Such a long, hard time.

He lifted his gaze from the box and tried to clear his mind. There were kids playing soccer, running and shouting at each other as their family and friends watched on and chatted. There was Dylan, the man of the hour, who was celebrating his fortieth birthday. Dylan had his own struggles, with depression rather than alcohol, and who could blame him? This drought was taking everything away from him. Now, the bank was threatening foreclosure, and yet Dylan could muster a smile for his friends and family. Surely Lachie could last one more day without a drink.

He swallowed hard. His gaze found his brother Darcy, and he remembered why he had decided to sober up in the first place.

Because Daniel, their father, had been a no-good, child-abusing, wife-beating drunk, and there was no way in hell Lachie wanted to be anything like him.

The fire of resolve burned through him and he reached instead for a can of Coke.

The sugary, black drink had become his new addiction. He knew how many calories it contained and that he was becoming softer around the middle because of it, but at least it didn't make him say and do stupid things. His drinking had cost him too much. It was not going to cost him anything else.

"Lachie." Darcy beckoned his brother over to where he stood at the barbecue, turning sausages.

After slugging a mouthful of cola, Lachie walked over to join him.

"I hope you're not burning them," Lachie said, looking at the smoking plate filled with sausages.

"Do me a favour and start putting the beef patties on?" Darcy motioned to an esky next to them.

Lachie nodded and retrieved the meat. There had to be a hundred people attending the party today, and there was easily enough meat in the esky to feed them twice over.

"Who supplied the meat?" Lachie asked as he started pulling the patties apart and placing them on the plate where Darcy was making room.

"Johnno, the butcher donated it," Darcy said.

"I thought he was struggling? There has to be a few hundred dollars' worth in there."

"He offered, said it was for a good cause. I think he was right. Look at how the community has come together."

Lachie looked out again at all the people. Many were graziers like him and Darcy who were working their families land. Lachie had sent the Brigadier Station stock to agistment properties years ago, when they'd thought the drought would only last a few years. Ten years on, it was still dry, with only the occasional sprinkle of rain to tease them.

It was as bad as it could get. Brigadier Station was holding on by the tips of its fingers. Many had not been so lucky.

Lachie needed to think of other things. He didn't want to talk about the weather today. "I haven't seen Meghan yet. How is your wife doing? Got her pregnant yet?"

Darcy's face paled and his hands stilled.

"Shit, what'd I say?" Lachie said.

Darcy looked at his brother; his usually bright blue eyes had turned dark. "She's not here. She's avoiding anywhere with kids, especially babies."

Lachie followed his gaze to a circle of women who were all nursing babies of various ages from newborns to just crawling toddlers.

"She had another miscarriage last week. This one makes three."

Lachie swore on an exhale and laid a hand on Darcy's shoulder. "I'm sorry. I didn't know."

"No one does. Not even Mum," Darcy said. "I flew her to Townsville to see a specialist who ran some tests. Turns out she has bicornate uterus. Which basically means it's shaped like a heart and didn't form normally."

"Wow." Lachie had seen all sorts of reproductive problems over the years in cows and remembered one time the vet had diagnosed a small pelvic area being the reason why one of their cows had miscarried her calf. The heifer had lost too much blood after the ordeal and Lachie'd had to put the poor thing out of its misery. "Is there anything they can do? Surgery or drugs?"

"Now that we know, she can be monitored. She gets pregnant easily enough; it's just keeping it that's hard."

"That's got to be tough. I'm so sorry for you." Lachie couldn't imagine what his brother and sister-in-law must be going through. They both wanted kids so much and had been trying for a long time. He couldn't imagine how hard losing one pregnancy must be, let alone three of them.

They were quiet for a while as they flipped meat and concentrated on cooking. Lachie had decided children were not on the books for him. He liked them well enough and would enjoy being an uncle, but the closest he had come to having a family had ended when his fiancée had left him at the altar. For his brother.

Lachie had forgiven Meghan for that and was happy she had found such love with Darcy. He knew that she had chosen the better man and even though they were dealing with these problems now, they would make it through together, no matter what.

"Lachie," Dylan's voice cut through his daydream. He had found him in the crowd and they shook hands in greeting. "Thanks for coming over."

"Wouldn't have missed it. It's quite a turnout." Lachie noted his neighbour's hollow cheeks and the way his baggy clothes hung from his thin frame.

"I wasn't expecting so many people. Maddie said it would be a small gathering." Dylan's smile was full of heart and his voice was choked with emotion. "I feel so lucky to have such great mates. It's been a hard few years."

Lachie nodded. "It sure has been. We've just got to keep working and pray for rain."

Dylan turned his head up to the sky. Not a rain cloud in sight.

Everyday Lachie checked but there was never a bloody cloud in that endless blue sky. "It's raining in Darwin. Maybe it'll come down here."

"Nah," Dylan shook his head, "the weather forecast shows it going back to sea."

"Damn." Lachie said. "Even a sprinkle would be a welcome change."

Stories were shared and people caught up on town events over steak burgers, sausages, and hearty serves of coleslaw and potato bake. Lachie chatted with his neighbours and discussed all things from the drought—forecasted to continue for at least another year—to why he hadn't been to the pub recently.

"I've given up the grog." He repeated, this time to the publican himself.

"Really?" The old man's weathered face fell. "Damn, you were the only business I could rely on."

Lachie frowned, unsure if the man was joking or not. Probably not. It was no secret that the pub had been Lachie's second home since he was old enough to drink, and even before that.

He turned his gaze, eager for somebody, anybody to save him from feeling guilty about sobering up.

"I think I'll go play soccer with the kids," he said and hurried away from the old man.

There were enough children running around the dusty paddock to make up more than two teams. Even the youngest of the rural offspring were running after their older siblings and friends as the soccer ball was kicked between booted feet.

Lachie watched them as they shrieked at each other and tried to steal the ball. He recognised Emma, Dylan's daughter, just as they spotted him and yelled at him to join in.

He jogged onto the field and followed the ball until he saw an opening, then took off through the gap with the ball just ahead of his feet. He lasted about five paces before an older boy, tall and stocky for his age, knocked into him from the side, driving him to the ground.

Lachie went down hard, his stomach landing directly on the boy's size 11 steel capped boot. The pain around his middle was immediate and debilitating. He couldn't stop the groan that escaped him.

❧

Abigail watched the children playing on the dusty open paddock. Her six-year-old daughter, Hannah, was playing alongside her friends, her shorts dirty and her blonde hair coming loose from its ponytail.

The noise on the field changed. The man who had been playing with them, who she had noticed from a distance but hadn't recognised, was lying on the ground, curled up in the foetal position. Abbie started running towards the group, her medical instincts taking over just as her daughter started running towards her.

They met halfway.

"I don't know what's wrong with him, Mum. He got pushed and fell over; now he won't get up. None of us know why. It wasn't that hard." Emma said.

Abbie smiled at her daughter and thanked her before continuing on to her patient.

As soon as she was close enough, she assessed the hulk of the man on the ground. He was clutching at his lower abdomen. She crouched next to him, ignoring the hard earth under her bare knees. How she wished she had opted for pants instead of the summer dress she was wearing.

"My name is Abbie and I'm a nurse," she said in her best bedside voice. "Can you tell me what happened?"

He turned his face to her and she swallowed. The pain was written all over his beautifully chiselled jawbone and blue eyes. So blue. So familiar, somehow.

"I landed on the kids boot when I tripped over. So much pain."

Abbie looked at the boot in question, then up at the rather guilty looking red face of a large boy hovering nearby. She turned her attention to the man's belly. "Have you had any past injuries or operations 'round here?"

He humphed. "I grew up on the farm. I've had all manner of injuries and accidents over the years."

"Lachie, are you okay?

Abbie looked up and recognised Darcy McGuire. Maddie had introduced her to Darcy earlier when she'd first arrived.

"I don't know. It hurts," the injured man replied.

"Lachie is that your name?" Abbie asked.

Darcy responded. "Yeah. He's my brother."

Abbie nodded, then turned to her patient. "Lachie, I'm just going to touch you very gently. Tell me where it hurts."

Lachie nodded and moved his arms out of the way.

She placed her hands on top of his shirt and gently applied pressure. He moaned and grabbed at her wrists. The pressure of his calloused hands wasn't enough to cause any real pain, but reminded her she was dealing with a man with far more strength than she had.

"Sorry." He loosened his grip.

"It's okay. Do you mind if I unbutton your shirt to make sure there is no bruising?"

He nodded. "That's fine."

She went to work on the buttons.

"Can I do something?" Darcy asked, his voice tense with worry. "I could get him some painkillers?"

"No." Lachie's voice was adamant. "I can't take anything."

His eyes sought Abbie's and she nodded, understanding there was more to the story.

"Probably better he doesn't take anything until we know what's going on." She smiled up at Darcy.

Lachie's pale skin was solid under her touch. As she moved the sides of his shirt apart, she saw there was no obvious bruising. She ran through the list of possibilities in her mind.

"And there's been no recent injuries?"

"He was in a quad bike accident," Darcy said when his brother remained silent. "He broke some ribs and hurt some tendons. The doctors suspected spinal injuries but he got the all-clear."

Abbie pursed her lips. "How long ago was this?"

"A couple of years."

"And you haven't been feeling sick recently or having any pain?" she asked Lachie.

"No, I've been fine. It wasn't until I fell that anything hurt."

She buttoned his shirt back up then turned to Darcy. "We need to take him to hospital."

Lachie moaned and wiped a hand over his face. "I'll be fine." He moved to sit, but the grimace on his face told her she was making the right decision.

Darcy nodded. "I can take him."

"It's a long drive," she said, thinking about every bump and pothole that stood between them and the township of Julia Creek. "I'll take him in my car. I live in town anyway, and the hospital is short-staffed today. I can monitor him during the trip."

Darcy looked between Lachie and Abbie. Lachie's nod of consent was all it took for Darcy to agree to the plan.

"It's probably nothing. You stay here and enjoy the party," Lachie said to his brother.

"Yeah, right," Darcy muttered under his breath as an older lady came to kneel beside them.

"Mum, I'm okay," Lachie said, and Abbie watched as he put on a stoic expression.

"No, you're not." She turned to Abbie. "You're the new nurse, aren't you?"

"I am." Abbie introduced herself and explained the situation. "I'll call when we know what's happened. There's really no need to come."

"Thank you. I'm Harriet, his mother." She said then turned back to Lachie and squeezed his hand. "Are you sure you don't want me to come?"

"Yes, Mum. I need you to stay on the station and feed the chooks anyway."

The plan was agreed to, and Lachie was helped into Abbie's Land Cruiser. She arranged pillows and towels around him to make him as comfortable as possible.

Her daughter climbed into her booster seat beside him. Abbie glanced at Hannah who seemed to be taking it all in.

"Honey, we're just going to take Lachie to the hospital in town, and then we'll go home. Okay?"

Hannah smiled at her mum as though this was another great adventure. "Okay."

Abbie then turned her attention to her patient and placed a hand on his finely muscled arm. "I've made you as comfortable as I can, but I won't lie. it will be a long trip into town. I'll be going slow to minimise any bumps."

Lachie nodded and looked into her eyes. His were so blue. He gave her a weak smile of thanks.

Shutting the door softly, she heard her daughter say, "My name is Hannah. I'm six."

Abbie walked around the car to the driver's side. "I'll call you with an update as soon as I have one." Abbie promised Darcy and Harriet who were waiting anxiously nearby. She slid into the car, started the ignition and with a reassuring smile at them started driving slowly along the bumpy, dirt driveway.

Before they had even left the property, Hannah had Lachie engaged in a deep conversation about school, what she was learning, and what it had been like when Lachie had attended the public school many years before.

"After my youngest brother, Noah, was born, we got a Governess to teach us," he explained.

"What's a governess?" Hannah asked.

"It's a teacher who lives with you."

"Oh, like Paige." Hannah nodded. "She's our friend in Hughenden."

Abbie joined the conversation. "Only she's not the governess anymore because she married Logan, the kid's father, so now she's their step-mum."

"Is that Logan from Currawilla Station?"

Their eyes locked in the rear-view mirror. "Do you know him?"

Lachie laughed. "We went to the same boarding school. I actually attended their wedding. Is that where I met you?"

"No, I didn't go to it. I've only met her recently," Abbie said. "They did a School of the Air camp here with the Julia Creek school kids about six months ago. It was just after we moved here."

Lachie nodded but a frown creased his handsome face. "Then how do I know you? You seem so familiar."

"You do too." She shook her head. How could she forget such a gorgeous man? She doubted she would ever forget him now, especially after the dramatic events of today. "I don't know. I'm usually so good with remembering faces and names."

"Mummy remembers all her patients. We meet them on the street sometimes," Hannah explained. "It gets kind of annoying."

"I know what that's like," Lachie said in a loud whisper. "Whenever I go to town, I always bump into a lot of people I know. It makes what should be a quick trip take all day."

Hannah laughed and Lachie smiled fondly at her. Abbie's heart cartwheeled. It was a rare man who made such an effort with her daughter. The guys she'd dated in Brisbane had never been interested in meeting Hannah, let alone playing dad to her. After a while, Abbie had stopped dating altogether and concentrated on being the best nurse and mother she could.

But she always had niggling doubt... was Hannah missing out not having a father or a male role model in her life? Single parent guilt sliced through her as it often did when she let herself dwell on the what-ifs and if-onlys.

After what seemed like an eternity on the road, she

spotted the sign welcoming them to the small outback town of Julia Creek. Abbie opened her phone and hit the speed dial for the hospital.

"Jill, it's Abbie. I'll be arriving in about five minutes with an emergency patient. He's a male with pain in his abdomen after a fall playing soccer, and his name is-"

Jill cut her off. "You've got Lachie McGuire. I know; his mum called. We're ready for him."

"Great see you soon." Abbie disconnected the call and took the turn towards the hospital. "We're almost there."

CHAPTER 2

*L*achie groaned as he shifted and manoeuvred his way out of Abbie's car and into the waiting wheelchair. The pain had only worsened on the journey, but at least the company had helped to shift his focus.

He felt Hannah's small hand curl around his arm and he concentrated on putting on a brave face for her. Lachie never gave much attention to young children. He didn't see many of them in his day-to-day life. But after spending the last hour with Hannah, chatting about school, sport, and families, he had come to learn a lot about what interested a six-year-old girl. She was sweet and compassionate, like her mother.

His attention turned to Abbie who was walking beside him, discussing his symptoms with the doctor. She was so beautiful and when she touched him … if he died today, he was grateful to have received good care from such an angel.

Another stab of pain crested through his middle. Yes,

this was the end. He would finally pay for his past mistakes and die from whatever horror had been inflicted on him.

They were shown to an examination room and he was helped onto the bed with its stiff white sheets. One sniff, and the antiseptic smell reminded him of those terrible weeks he had spent in Townsville Hospital. After three days unconscious, he had woken up in excruciating pain with two broken ribs, minor burns, and nerve damage in his arms and legs. He had hoped never to step foot into a hospital again, at least not as a patient.

And now he'd been hurt playing soccer, being healthy with not even a drop of liquor in him. Another of life's cruel tricks.

"How's the pain now?" the doctor asked as he pushed cold hands against Lachie's abdomen. At least Abbie's soft hands had been warm.

"Lachie."

He turned at Abbie's voice and gazed again at that beautiful face, with her ivory skin and grey eyes. Hannah had blue eyes; she must take after her father.

"Lachie," she repeated, "how's your pain on a scale of one to ten, ten being the worst?"

He shifted under the doctor's insistent probing. "Ten."

"We'll give him something for that before we run those tests," the doctor said.

"Wait." Abbie stopped the doctor as he started to turn away, then placed her hands on either side of Lachie's face.

That got his attention.

Her voice was quiet as though she only wanted him to

hear her. "Back at the station, you said no to painkillers. Why? Do you have an allergy?"

Lachie looked at the doctor, then at Hannah. She was studying a chart on the wall, her hand still wrapped around his arm.

He could so easily say yes to the drugs that would bring him oblivion and rescue him from the pain he was suffering. But, in the seemingly unlikely chance that he survived this ordeal, he would suffer even more. Sobering up had been hard enough the first time; he didn't think he could go through it again.

He swallowed hard, his voice shallow and husky when he answered. "I'm a recovering alcoholic."

She nodded, and he was surprised to see no judgment in her eyes. She let go of his face and turned to consult with the doctor.

He strained to hear what was being said when Hannah tapped his shoulder. "Have you ever had to stay overnight in hospital before? I heard the food is really bad. Is it true they give you jelly? I like jelly. Well, I like strawberry jelly. I tried orange jelly once, but I didn't like that. What flavour is green jelly? I like the colour green, but I like purple better. I wouldn't mind trying purple jelly. I like grapes so I'd probably like grape jelly. What's your favourite flavour?"

Lachie shook his head. "Um, my favourite flavour jelly is strawberry too. I like it with ice cream."

Hannah's face lit up with a smile as though he had just agreed to take her to Disneyland. "Me too. I love ice cream—"

"Hannah," Abbie interrupted, "why don't you go into

the waiting room and play with the toys. I'll meet you there soon."

"Okay." Hannah bent over then and kissed Lachie's cheek. "My mum will look after you. She's a great nurse."

"Thanks, squirt." He gave her his bravest smile and watched her skip from the room. She seemed quite at home here, and he wondered how much time she had spent in hospitals over her short life.

"Sorry about her. She probably talked your ear off," Abbie said.

"It was a great distraction. She's a wonderful kid."

Pride stretched her full lips into a smile. Oh, how he'd like to taste those lips …

"So, the doctor is going to perform an ultrasound first and see if he can find anything. Because of your addiction, he's going to hold off giving you any pain relief for as long as he can. Unfortunately, most drugs are a form of codeine and can be a trigger for addicts."

"Yeah, I've heard the spiel in AA."

"Well, I'm glad you listened. You must take sobriety very seriously."

"Of course I do." He frowned. Why wouldn't he take it seriously? Every day he had to fight not to drink. It would be too easy to start again.

She glanced around the room, they were alone for the first time.

"How long have you been sober?" she asked.

"Ten months."

"Good for you. That's a big achievement." Her words made him smile through his pain.

"Thanks."

"You'll need to remove your shirt and unbutton your jeans so we can perform an ultrasound on your abdomen. Do you want me to help?"

She was all professionalism, yet he still felt himself squirm. He stopped abruptly as the pain started. He gave a small nod, knowing he wouldn't be able to undress on his own and hating being so helpless. Still, if anyone had to undress him, he didn't mind it being this woman.

She unbuttoned his shirt, her eyes on the job, and he took the opportunity to study her at such close proximity. Her skin was pale and freckles covered her nose, although they were mostly covered by makeup. He wondered how dark they would be free from foundation. She had long lashes, and her brows had a lovely curve.

He sucked in a breath as her fingers reached for his belt buckle, and he breathed in her scent. Feminine and oh-so sexy.

"Can you lean forward?" Her voice had a huskiness to it and he wondered if just maybe he affected her the way she affected him.

He moved as instructed and, when her fingers brushed over his exposed skin, he felt sensation in parts of his body that weren't the cause of his admission.

He looked up at her face, just mere inches away. She was biting her lip. He turned away before the urge to bite it for her overtook him.

Except his gaze fell to her chest. Her low-cut summer dress gaped open to his view, and he could see the exposed tops of her rounded breasts and the lace of her white bra. A small brown mole sat above her bra line on her right breast, and he frowned at the sense of déjà vu that came over him. Before he could think too much on it, she laid him back, carefully folded his discarded shirt, and put it at the bottom of the bed.

He opened his mouth to say something, anything, but the doctor and nurse rattled in with a portable ultrasound machine.

"Now lie back. The gel will be cold," the doctor instructed as the bed was lowered. Lachie cringed and closed his eyes, then a soft hand took his. He looked up to see Abbie smiling down at him, her fingers entwined with his. He looked down at her left hand. No ring. Maybe there was hope after all.

$\sim$

Abbie prided herself on delivering the best possible care and bedside manner but also not getting too involved or attached to her patients. For some reason, she was letting that all fly out the window when it came to Lachie McGuire. When she had taken off his shirt, she had felt something—an attraction. It was brewing between them with every look, every touch. It had been so long since she had been with a man, since she had wanted to even think about a relationship, but now Lachie was messing with her mind and making her want all sorts of crazy things. To do all sorts of crazy things.

The doctor pulled her from her fantasy. "You were right, Nurse Forsyth."

She studied the screen in front of them. The ultrasound wand was on Lachie's middle.

"Incisional hernia." She breathed out her earlier diagnosis.

"A hernia?" Lachie questioned loudly.

"It looks like the bowel has pushed through a weakened spot in the abdominal muscle," the doctor explained.

Abbie squeezed his hand. "It could have been weakened during your motorbike accident, then today's accident ruptured it."

"Okay. So, can you fix it?" Lachie looked between the medical professionals surrounding him.

"Since it's causing so much pain, we have to operate immediately before it causes any more damage." The doctor looked down at a clipboard he was holding. "Normally we would transfer you to Townsville, where they could do keyhole surgery, but I don't think we have enough time. We'll have to open you up." The doctor continued to explain the risks of this type of surgery and what kind of recovery he could expect.

Abbie watched as Lachie's eyes widened in alarm. "You'll be alright. Doctor Ferguson has performed this type of surgery many times, and even though recovery will take a few weeks, it will be far less painful than what you're feeling now."

His eyes were wide when he turned to her. "Will you be in the operating theatre too?"

Abbie nodded and smiled, knowing she'd have to ask the doctor and figure out what to do with Hannah, but also sure she had to be in the theatre. Hernia surgery could be risky and she wanted to make sure Lachie came out fine and healthy on the other side. "Trust me. You'll be alright. I'll be with you every step."

"I trust you," he said and she felt a shiver of anticipation.

Harriet and Darcy arrived in time to see Lachie before surgery and conveniently offered to look after Hannah so Abbie could assist with Lachie's surgery. As she scrubbed in, Abbie focused her thoughts on the surgery, what needed to be done, and what role she would play. Those years as an ER nurse really paid off at times like these, and she was grateful for her varied nursing experience.

Having her parents there to look after Hannah was the only reason she had been able to work the long shifts in the Brisbane hospitals. Of course, that had meant letting them help with Hannah's upbringing and early education. As much as Abbie loved and respected her parents, she didn't want her child raised with the upper-brow, better-than-everyone-else view her parents held.

It had been one of the reasons Abbie had rebelled and gone into nursing. The reason she had taken that road trip to the Birdsville races.

After she'd finished preparing, she pushed through the door and into the tiny, rarely used operating theatre.

She watched as Lachie was rolled in. They had changed him into a hospital gown. A blue cap covered his thick brown hair, and he was tucked in with warm blankets.

"Hi." She hovered over him and spoke through her face mask.

He looked up, and his face relaxed as he recognised her. "Abbie."

The anaesthetist rolled his chair over and chatted to Lachie about the surgery and the anaesthesia he would be receiving. When he was ready to administer it, Abbie returned to Lachie's side.

"Are you alright?" she asked.

"Don't leave me." His voice was pleading. She often saw patients like this, their bravado stripped away to reveal their vulnerability.

"I won't. I promise I'll be beside you the whole time and here when you wake up."

He shot her a smile of thanks. "Okay, then I'm ready." He breathed deeply before the anaesthesia was put into a drip and flowed into the cannula she had placed in his arm earlier. Then she watched as his eyelids drooped lower and lower until he was asleep.

"Nurse," the doctor said, drawing her attention from her sleeping patient. "We're ready to start."

CHAPTER 3

"Lachie, wake up. It's all over." Abbie patted his hand and waited for him to come to.

His eyes flickered open briefly then closed again. The anaesthesia hadn't worn off, and he was still dopey from its affects. The machine between them continued to beep reassuringly. It was the only noise in the small recovery room.

She stroked his big, work-roughened hand with her fingertips and gazed at the giant of a man. Up close like this, she was able to fully appreciate the sharp angles of his face. He had a strong jaw, a pouty bottom lip, and a hint of a dimple in his chin. He was the kind of good-looking that could sweep an unsuspecting female off her feet and straight into bed.

Taking a deep breath, she contemplated the likelihood of anyone ever sweeping her off her feet.

Finally, he stirred again and opened his eyes. "Abbie?"

"I'm right here," she said.

His blue-eyed gaze locked on hers, and she felt it again. That attraction, the sense of familiarity.

"You didn't leave me." A satisfied smile curled the edges of his mouth. God, it was sexy.

Even in the hospital gown, hooked up to a drip and machines, he still managed to look sexy as hell. She could only imagine how he would look if he actually tried.

She tried to keep her brain focused. "The surgery was a success. You're going to be just fine."

He blinked. "You're beautiful." His words were slurred, and she smiled to herself. It was perfectly normal behaviour post-surgery. He didn't know what he was saying and he likely wouldn't remember any of it. "I love you."

She couldn't help but giggle. It wasn't the first time a patient had declared their undying love for her post-surgery. "You're going to be just fine."

"I love you, Abbie. I want to marry you." His eyes were so open and honest that she almost believed him.

"Oh yeah? What about Hannah?" She played along.

"I love Hannah too. She's wonderful. Just like her mummy." The slurring had lessened now. "Except her eyes. She has her father's eyes."

She gazed into those bright blue eyes and gulped. Eyes the exact same as Hannah's. Even down to the tiny brown flecks. What were the odds?

"Your mother and brother are in the waiting room. I'll go and get them for you." She made to stand but he tugged on her arm.

"Thank you, Abbie," he said, then raised her hand to

his lips and brushed his warm lips over her skin. Her heart pounded.

"I'll be back in a minute." She fled the room. Away from the feelings and emotions he stirred in her. She wasn't looking for love. She and Hannah were doing so well by themselves, and she couldn't screw that up. Even if she was ready, the last man she should be thinking of dating was an alcoholic cowboy. It would never work.

Would it?

∽

"It was an incisional hernia, but we managed to repair all the damage and stitch it back together without any complications," the doctor explained. "You will need to rest for at least a week, then light duties for another three weeks."

"Thank you, Doctor," his mother said and squeezed Lachie's hand. Darcy stood behind her, a look of relief on his face. Lachie remembered that look. Darcy had worn it after the accident, like he felt responsible for causing it. He must be feeling guilty all over again.

"So, when can I get out of here?" Lachie asked.

Abbie shifted next to the doctor. How was it possible for a woman to look that good in hospital scrubs? Damn, he must still be high from those drugs. He remembered Abbie holding his hand when he woke up, but his memory was all a bit fuzzy until his mother came in.

"You can leave in the morning, but I'd like you to stay close by at least for a week."

"We live at Brigadier Station. It's the best part of a forty-minute drive," Harriet said, worry lining her voice.

The doctor pursed his lips and looked at Lachie. "Do you have family or friends in town you can stay with?"

Lachie shook his head. His friends were all old drinking buddies from the pub. Not the type he could stay with unless he wanted to fall into old habits, which he definitely did not.

"He can stay with me," Abbie announced, surprising herself. "Who better to look after him than a nurse?"

Lachie looked at her questioningly, but she nodded at him. "It's just for a week. It'll be fine."

Was she trying to convince him or herself.

Lachie felt his pulse spike and was grateful the machines were turned off. He wouldn't mind spending a week with Abbie. She was the type of woman he would like to get to know better. He enjoyed Hannah's company too. It would mean that he wouldn't be able to mope about feeling sorry for himself as long as Hannah was around.

The doctor nodded enthusiastically. "Excellent. You will be in great hands. Nurse Forsyth is one of the best nurses I've ever had the pleasure of working with."

Lachie watched Abbie's reaction to his words. A soft blush tinged her cheeks.

When the doctor had left, Harriet turned to Abbie. "Are you sure that's not an inconvenience? You must have a busy life with work and your daughter."

Abbie shook her head. "Not at all. I have a couple of days off anyway, and Hannah will be at school."

Harriet relented with a smile. "Okay. I'll come and

visit as much as I can." She patted Lachie's hand. "You better behave yourself."

Abbie laughed a high-pitched melody. It was the first time he had heard it, and he smiled. Laughing suited her.

Abbie turned to him. "If you're all set, I'll come back and pick you up in the morning."

He nodded, wondering how he could express his gratitude. "Thank you. For everything."

"No problem." She smiled and said her goodbyes to his family.

A cheeky smile spread over his mother's face as she turned and looked at him.

"What?" he asked slowly.

"She likes you."

Darcy moved to sit in a spare chair next to Harriet. "I think Mum's right."

"Nah, she's just doing her job." Lachie brushed it off. "Besides, she could do better than me anyway."

"Give yourself more credit," Darcy said. "You've come a long way."

"Still a long way to go before I'm worthy of a woman like her," Lachie said as his mother and brother gave each other a knowing look. "I've got to live with her for the next week. Leave it alone, you two."

"Okay," they both agreed at the same time with a smile.

Lachie threw his head back and groaned.

It was going to be an interesting week.

～

"Here we are," Abbie said as she turned off the car's igni-

tion and unclipped her seatbelt. Lachie pulled his attention away from her to look at the little, white
weatherboard house. He noted its convenient position,
on the same road as the primary school and around the
corner from the hospital. Walking distance, except when
travelling with a patient who had just had major
surgery.

"It's nice," he said as he opened the car door and tried
to get out unassisted. Before he got very far though, Abbie
was there, gripping his arm and supporting him as he
awkwardly climbed out. "Thanks."

Her arm curled around his waist, and he put his over
her shoulder. She was petite against him, at least a foot
shorter, but she surprised him with her strength. They
managed to get up the steps and to the front door where
she unlocked the door and helped him over the threshold.

"Let's get you on the couch," she said and directed him
into the open-plan living, dining, and kitchen. He slid into
the comfortable fabric couch and sighed.

"Are you in pain? I can get you some medicine." She
rattled the paper bag which contained the packet of non-
addictive pain-relievers the doctor had prescribed.
Lachie'd managed a few hours' sleep last night after
having swallowed one, but its effects had been fleeting.

He shook his head. "No, I'll save them for when it gets
really bad." If she thought he was trying to be brave for
her, he wasn't. She had already seen him at his weakest so
he had nothing to prove now.

He watched as she put the bag on the kitchen counter
then disappeared down the hall, returning a moment later
with pillows which she carefully arranged around him.

When she was done, she stood back and put her hands on her hips. "How about a cup of tea?"

"That would be great." He agreed more to give her something to do than because he wanted one. As she bustled about in the kitchen, he looked around the room. It was sparsely decorated with just one photo of Hannah as a baby on the wall. "How long have you lived here?"

"Since we got here six months ago," she said. "The house is owned by the hospital and let out to staff."

"Where did you move from? You're a city girl, right?"

"Is it that obvious?" She shot him a smile. "We're from Brisbane."

Abbie brought over a tray of biscuits, a milk jug, sugar bowl, and two cups of tea. She placed them on the table beside him before sitting down opposite.

He dosed his tea with sugar and took a sip. "It's your skin. Too pale for a country girl."

She pressed her hand against her cheek. "You can blame my father for that. He's Scottish, and as fair as they come."

"Scottish, really? What brought him to Australia?" Lachie relaxed into his nest of pillows and waited for her to answer.

"Love." She shrugged. "He met my mother while she was travelling around Europe and then came back with her."

"Really? She didn't want to stay there?" he asked.

"No. He was pretty happy to immigrate to a warmer climate."

"Have you ever been there? To Scotland?"

She nodded. "We regularly went over while I was

growing up. We had quite a few white Christmases. I haven't been overseas since I started uni though."

"You don't want to take Hannah over, for a holiday?"

"Maybe one day, but it's a long way for a little girl." Abbie sipped her drink, and he watched as she curled a leg under her.

"She's a great kid. Very talkative." Lachie grinned.

Abbie laughed. "Yes, she is. She would talk to anyone about anything. It worries me sometimes."

He furrowed his brows. "What do you mean?"

"You know 'stranger danger'?"

He nodded slowly. When you lived in a small community, strangers didn't stay strangers for long, but he saw the reasoning behind it. He had watched enough crime shows to understand how prevalent kidnappings were in large cities, and he wouldn't wish that on any parent.

Abbie sighed. "Still, she's the reason I met Maddie and Dylan."

He cocked his head to the side, signalling for her to explain.

"Hannah went up to Jamie in the supermarket one day and started playing with him. That's when Maddie and I started talking, and she invited us out to the station. We've been good friends ever since. Jamie's like a little brother to her now."

Lachie had only spent a brief amount of time with his neighbours' son, and that was when he'd still been a baby. He remembered Meghan had been particularly fond of the little boy. "That's great. I imagine it must get lonely as an only child. I'm the oldest of three brothers."

"I'm an only child too, so I know what she's going

through. It is lonely, but it's just the way it is." Her voice was heavy with something. Regret?

"So, Hannah's father …?" He wanted to know more and didn't know how to be polite about it.

"He's not around." Her face clouded over, ending the conversation. "Never has been."

Lachie sipped his tea in awkward silence. No more talking about the father—check.

He was about to apologise when there was a tapping on the door. "That will be your mum. She said she was on her way."

He smiled and finished his tea. His mother would get Abbie talking. She could get anyone to open up, even him.

～

Harriet arrived with a bag of Lachie's things as well as containers of food and baking.

"It's the least I can do," she said as she handed them to Abbie. "After all, you're looking after my son."

Abbie took the food gratefully and went to work finding room for everything in the fridge. Well, at least she wouldn't have to worry about dinner tonight. Harriet had brought enough meals to last the week.

Harriet fussed over her son for a while, making sure he was comfortable and not in too much pain, not that there was much Abbie could give him if he was.

"So why did you leave Brisbane?" Harriet asked a short time later.

Abbie took a seat on the couch next to Lachie—the only other spare seat since Harriet was on the chair.

"I was working in the emergency department with long hours and lots of stress. Plus, I wasn't getting to spend much time with Hannah so when I heard about this job I decided it would be a nice change from the rush of the city."

"Yes, I think you'll find Julia Creek quite different." Harriet nodded. "How long will you be staying?"

"Indefinitely. Hannah's enjoying it here. She loves her school and new friends," Abbie said, smiling. "We'll return at some point, I guess. But who knows when?"

"And Hannah's father? Has he come to visit yet?" Harriet asked inquisitively.

Abbie shifted. "He's not in the picture. It's just me and Hannah."

Harriet frowned. "I'm sorry to hear that."

Abbie shrugged like it really didn't matter. Lots of kids grew up with only one parent. Hannah seemed okay, didn't she?

"And your parents are still in Brisbane?" Lachie said, changing the subject.

She shot him a grateful look. "Yes, we used to live with them before we moved here. They were a great help when Hannah was little."

"I can imagine, especially with you being so young and with such a demanding job," Harriet said kindly. "They must be missing you now."

Abbie nodded. "They know they are welcome here anytime." Not that they would ever come out. The dusty outback was nothing like the glitzy lifestyle they were used to.

Lachie raised his hand to smother a yawn. He looked

exhausted. He probably hadn't slept much last night at the hospital with all the constant coming and going of hospital staff.

"You should have a sleep. I'll show you your room," Abbie said.

Lachie rubbed his hand over his face. "I normally hate to sleep during the day. Waste of sunlight hours, but if I don't lie down I'm pretty sure I'll fall asleep right here." He gingerly pushed himself off the couch, and Abbie caught his arm to steady him.

"I'll leave you to it then," Harriet said, standing. "Let me know if you need anything at all."

"Thanks, Mum." Lachie gave her a kiss on the cheek.

Abbie said her goodbyes and once Harriet had left, she put her arm around Lachie and helped him down the hall.

"That's the bathroom there." She pointed out the rooms as they passed. "And Hannah's room." She glanced in and was pleased to see the two single beds had been made and Hannah had tidied up before school this morning.

She guided Lachie into the room opposite. "This is my room and where you'll be sleeping."

He paused. "I didn't realise I was taking your bed. I'll be fine on the couch."

"It's alright. I'll sleep on the spare bed in Hannah's room." Abbie smiled reassuringly.

He made as if to argue his point, but she silenced him with a stern look. "There's no point arguing, Mr McGuire. Now get in there."

A smile creased his face and she felt his hard body

relax under her touch. She helped him to a sitting position on the bed.

Abbie pointed to his bag. "There are the things Harriet brought and there are some towels over there. Do you want to use the bathroom?"

He raised his eyebrows. "I'll be able to manage that part myself, thanks."

"I'm a nurse. I've seen it all before and much, much worse," she said with a sweet smile.

"I bet you have. But, no I'm fine." He kicked off his shoes and lay on the bed. She watched as he made himself comfortable on her side of the bed. "Are you going to watch me sleep too?" he asked with eyes closed.

She turned to the door. "Call out if you need anything."

She closed the door and leaned up against it. Images of him sleeping on her bed, between her sheets, his head on her pillow, swam though her mind. She shook her head and started back to the kitchen. Hannah would be home soon and she would be a welcome distraction.

∼

The sound of Hannah's soft girlish voice roused Lachie from a deep sleep. He yawned before pushing himself to a sitting position on the bed. The clock on the bedside table showed him he had slept though lunch and most of the afternoon. He felt better for it though.

Gingerly, he tested his pain by twisting at the middle. Yep, still there, though not as bad as it had been before his nap.

After going to the bathroom and splashing water on his face, he wandered to the kitchen.

Hannah looked up from the dining table where she was set up with paper and pencil. She jumped out of her seat and skipped towards him before snuggling into his side. "You're here."

He curled his arm around her.

"How did you sleep?" Abbie approached him, drying her hands on a tea towel.

"Great, thanks. Just what the nurse ordered." He smiled at her, then realised he was absentmindedly stroking Hannah's soft blonde hair. Blonde hair just as pale as her mother's.

Abbie's gaze slipped to her daughter. "Back to your homework now."

Hannah slowly peeled herself from Lachie's hip. "Will you help me with my spelling? It's really hard."

Lachie nodded and sat down next to her at the table.

"Dinner will be ready in about an hour. Would you like some coffee?" Abbie asked.

"Tea if you have any, thanks," he replied and watched as she reached into a cupboard. Her T-shirt pulled high enough to expose a strip of pale skin on her back.

He gulped back the feelings it stirred in him.

"Lachie?" Hannah demanded his attention. "What's this word?"

He focused on the worksheet in front of him and for the next few minutes, he and Hannah recited a list of spelling words. After delivering his tea, Abbie gave his arm a light squeeze of thanks.

Once her books were put away, Hannah asked if he'd

play a board game with her. Lachie looked to Abbie for permission. He would gladly spend all evening playing with the kid; she was funny and sweet. It was a nice change from evenings of serious adult conversation and routine with his mother.

"How about you have your shower first, then you can play a round of Guess Who?"

Hannah squealed. "I love Guess Who! Will you play with me?"

Lachie nodded. "Sure, squirt, after your shower."

Hannah trotted off down the hall, and Lachie swallowed the last of his tea.

"Thanks for that. She's always been the centre of attention, so if she gets too much, just let me know."

"She's great. I don't mind at all." He stood and walked to the sink where he cleaned his cup and put it in the drying rack. Then he turned to Abbie who was slicing cucumber. "Can I help?"

Abbie looked him over. "Are you feeling okay? You should be resting."

"I feel fine. Let me help you."

After a brief pause she nodded at the fridge. "There's lettuce in there. Can you wash it for me?"

He retrieved the head of lettuce, unwrapped it, and started rinsing it in the sink. "I haven't had store-bought lettuce for ages."

"Really?"

"Mum grows them. She's got a real green thumb and plants all sorts of vegetables. It's hard with the heat, but she does it somehow."

"It must be great living out there and being self-sufficient. It's like a lottery going into the supermarket here. Maybe they'll have a lettuce and maybe they'll have apples. No guarantees though. Then, if they do have it, the prices are astounding. And the meat." She pulled a face.

"Only you townsfolk need to buy the meat," he teased. "The butcher has good cuts. We sell him some of ours when we can."

Lachie thought about the dwindling herd that remained on Brigadier Station. Most were still on agistment in greener pastures, the drought making feed hard to come by in the region. The few heifers left were barely worth killing for the meat on their bones. Their chickens had become a more frequent meal, and although the change was nice, he was getting sick of having eggs at almost every meal.

He glanced at the oven where something was cooking in a casserole dish. "Is that Mum's pasta bake?"

Abbie laughed. "It's covered in aluminium foil; how on earth can you tell?"

He sniffed the air. "Smells like my childhood."

Their eyes met and held.

"Where do you want me to put this?" He motioned to the lettuce. She handed him a salad bowl and he was careful to ensure their fingers didn't touch.

"Guess Who time," Hannah said, dressed in pyjama shorts and a T-shirt with a pink unicorn on it. Her long hair was wet and tangled down her back.

"Your hair needs drying and brushing first," Abbie said and looked around at the tomatoes and cucumbers she was in the middle of slicing. She was only halfway through.

"I'll brush her hair," Lachie offered. "I could do with a sit down."

"Alright," Abbie said and told him where to find everything he needed.

He soon found himself sitting at the table with Hannah in front of him. He used a towel to dry the long strands and then, as gently as he could, he tugged a comb through them.

She squirmed as the comb's teeth snagged on a knot but didn't cry out.

"Welcome to having a daughter." Abbie laughed.

He persevered and after a while found it strangely therapeutic. Hannah was chatting to him about school again and the games she and her friends liked to play while Abbie was finishing up in the kitchen. It was such a domestic scene and the feelings of contentment that overcame him, caught him off guard.

He was enjoying himself.

Dinner was served, and they chatted easily as they ate. Lachie couldn't help but feel right at home with these two. Even though he knew he didn't deserve to be happy, he yearned to be accepted and appreciated and with them, it felt as though he was.

After dinner and two rounds of Guess Who?, Hannah came back from having brushed her teeth and presented Lachie with a soft brown monkey.

"Who's this?" He studied the toy, which had seen better days. One of its ears had been chewed on and it was missing an eye.

"Mr Monkey. He'll help you sleep," she said.

He frowned. "Don't you need him with you?"

She shook her head. "You're sick. He'll help you get better. He always helps me."

Lachie's heart was full. He thanked the little girl for her thoughtfulness.

She put her arms around his neck and whispered into his ear, "Promise you'll be here when I wake up."

"I will be." He hugged her. "Thank you for Mr Monkey."

"Come on, Hannah. Bedtime," her mother said and Hannah unwrapped herself from him.

"Good night, Lachie."

"Good night, squirt."

He watched as Hannah took her mother's hand, and they walked down the hallway together.

He could get used to this life.

Shit.

CHAPTER 4

*I*t took Abbie twenty minutes to read to her daughter. Three stories just hadn't been enough.

"Can Lachie read to me tomorrow?" Hannah had asked, eyes full of hope and anticipation.

"Maybe. You'll have to ask him," she'd replied. Judging from the way he did everything Hannah asked, Abbie knew her daughter had Lachlan McGuire wrapped around her little finger. He was smitten, of that she was sure. She was already in lust with the man, but seeing how fondly he treated her child made her heart melt.

As she walked the few steps to the kitchen, she thought out her to-do list. Dishes, wipe down the table, and sweep under it. Hannah was a messy eater and always dropped food. She had enough house guests and didn't need any more, especially those of the bug, insect, or rodent variety.

Abbie stopped in her tracks when she saw the kitchen.

There was nothing sexier than a man doing housework and that was exactly what Lachie was doing.

The dishwasher was humming away and the tabletops were sparkling clean. Even the dining table had been wiped and, sure enough, under the table was food-free too.

"You cleaned up."

He turned to her, a tea towel and the casserole dish in his hands. "It's the least I could do."

"Thank you. But you're supposed to be taking it easy."

"I'm fine," he said.

With nothing to do, she sat in the nearest chair and sighed. "It's been a long time since I had any help. I really do appreciate it."

He turned that sexy smile on her and raised one eyebrow. "Well, I was hoping you could do something for me in return."

Her blood heated at the sight of his smouldering expression. "What's that?"

He put the dry dish away—in the right place, no less—and walked toward her. When he was mere inches away, he lifted his T-shirt revealing his smooth chest and pecs.

She bit the inside of her lip and tried not to stare at the scattering of dark hairs which led down, down, down.

His voice was teasing when he spoke. "Would you change my bandage?"

Her eyes shot to his face, and she felt her cheeks burn. "Oh, yeah, of course," she said, trying to compose herself. "Lie down on the bed."

He raised his eyebrows. Shit, even they were sexy.

"I mean the couch. Lie down on the couch."

She took her time gathering the fresh dressing and antiseptic ointment, all the while telling herself to get a grip and be professional.

She knelt beside him and carefully peeled off the old dressing. "It looks good. No infection there."

"That's a relief. I'm not keen to go back to hospital anytime soon."

She prepared the ointment. "This might sting a little." She touched it to the wound, and his muscles flexed but he stayed silent. It was as she'd expected; these rural men always put on a brave face.

She taped the new bandage on and rolled back on her heels. "All done. Tomorrow I'll dress it again after your shower." When he was warm and wet and slick ...

"Thanks." He pushed himself up and her hand automatically reached out to help him. He looked at her fingers wrapped around his bicep, then turned to look at her.

She dropped her arm and stood up. "I think I'll call it a night." Before she did or said something stupid. "You should too. But if you're not tired, you're welcome to stay up and watch TV or read."

He stayed sitting on the couch. "I don't suppose you have any good books I could borrow?"

"Not unless you like to read romance." She shared her daughter's love for literature, though she didn't expect Nora Roberts or Danielle Steele novels would be Lachlan's thing.

"I've never been much of a reader, unless you count *Outback* magazines and stock prices."

She picked up a magazine she remembered had

arrived in today's mail but she hadn't opened. "Must be your lucky day. Look what just arrived."

He grinned as he took the latest edition of *Outback* from her hands. "You have a subscription?" He ripped open the packaging and flicked through the must-have rural magazine.

"It helps me to understand my patients better. What challenges you guys are facing and how I can help."

"You're just full of surprises." The amused glint in his eyes did more damage than if he'd flashed her another grin.

She turned to leave. "Good night then. If you need anything, you know where I am."

"Good night, Abbie," he said as she started down the hall. "See you in the morning."

~

Lachie tossed and turned, unsure if it was because of the pain that he couldn't sleep or the visions of Abbie and the rosy pink blush that had tinted her otherwise pale skin the night before.

When she listened, her brow furrowed in concentration. When she laughed, a dimple flickered in her cheek. When she blushed, her eyes appeared a brilliant grey.

As the sky lightened, he sat on the edge of the bed and gathered his wits. He couldn't let his discomfort show, especially in front of Hannah. She was too young and innocent to learn of his past. He stared at her monkey on the bedside table and remembered the unassuming kindness of her action. He was a stranger to her, to both of them, and yet they had welcomed him into their home.

He pulled on a T-shirt and some rugby shorts before opening the door. As he passed, he glanced into Hannah's empty room. Both the beds looked slept in with the sheets still tousled and a collection of soft toys spread out on Hannah's bed. He wondered if she had slept alright without Mr Monkey.

"Morning," Abbie said as she looked up from tying her daughter's hair. Hannah was dressed in her school uniform—a polo shirt and navy shorts—while Abbie was still in her pyjamas. Her blonde hair was piled high in a knot on top of her head with loose tendrils brushing her long neck.

He smiled and greeted them before flicking on the electric kettle. If he couldn't have painkillers, he could at least have a strong cup of tea, his hit of caffeine. "Can I fix you a cuppa?" he asked Abbie.

"That would be great, thanks." She finished tying her daughter's hair. "Get your shoes on. Jenny will be here in a few minutes."

Hannah rushed down the hall to her room.

Abbie walked over to him. He took in her cotton shorts and oh-so-tight pale blue singlet. His pain was forgotten as all the blood in his body flooded to one organ. Turning quickly to the counter he asked, "Tea or coffee?"

"Tea please." She opened the fridge and pulled out the milk. "How did you sleep?"

"Fine, thanks." He lied.

She placed the milk on the table then turned and put

her hands on her hips, studying him. He tried to avoid looking at her, but it was like hiding from a hungry hawk.

She sighed. "Did you take some painkillers?"

He shook his head. "Not yet."

"Mum, where's my smelly pen? I want to take it for show and tell," Hannah said as she brushed past her mother, pushing her into Lachie's chest. He caught Abbie and held her, not wanting to let go. She smelled delicious, like ripe, freshly picked strawberries.

She cleared her throat and shifted gently away from his wound and out of his arms. "You know you aren't allowed toys at school. Now get your lunch box."

Lachie finished making their drinks and took his to the table. He sipped as he watched Abbie and Hannah finish their morning routine. Bag on her back, Hannah went to him and kissed his stubbly cheek. "Will you read to me tonight?"

He smiled. "I'd love to, squirt." He hugged her back, his heart full of emotion.

"Bye," she called as she bounded out the door to meet her friends.

"She walks to school?" he asked.

Abbie nodded and gulped her drink. "Her friend's mum collects a few kids on their way. The school is only a couple of minutes from here."

He nodded. "What are your shifts like at the hospital?"

"I've worked out a roster now that frees up most weekends and there is an after-school program she attends when I have to work." Abbie took some bread out of the fridge. "Would you like some toast? I'm addicted to Vegemite." She stopped and turned to him, an apology written all over her face. "I shouldn't have said that. I'm sorry."

"It's okay. I swapped mine for Coca-Cola and caffeine." He stood and took his cup to the sink. "Vegemite toast sounds like a good addiction to have. I might have a shower first though, see if the hot water helps."

She bit her lip, just like she had last night. It took all his energy not to take those lips in his own and kiss them until they started to swell.

She nodded, clearly unaware of the thoughts going through his mind. "Try not to get the wound wet." She pulled some plastic wrap from the drawer. "Stick some of this over the bandage before you get in, and I'll change it when you get out."

He took the wrapper.

"Do you want me to help?" She looked up at him though dark lashes.

He shook his head. If she touched him right then, there was no knowing what he would do.

"I'll be right, thanks," he said before heading down the hall. Perhaps it had better be a cold shower he took, rather than a hot one.

∼

Lachie's attempt at appearing fine didn't fool her. The hollows defining his cheekbones and the pallor beneath his tan suggested he should still be in bed.

Abbie opened the refrigerator door and started making a shopping list. It was important Lachie stay home and continue to rest. Judging by his pallor, she hoped he would be amenable to this idea. Although if he were like other country men, he would hate fuss, let alone being out of action. No doubt while she was making shopping lists, he was making to-do lists. Harriet had mentioned that Darcy was staying on to run the station while Lachie recovered with her.

She pulled out her phone and typed things into the notes app. Then she turned to the fridge and unclipped the stack of paperwork hanging on with magnets, which she had yet to deal with.

She signed the last of the forms just as Lachie's feet padded on the floorboards behind her.

She turned to see him wearing nothing but his blue jeans. His bare chest glistened with the residual water.

She focused her attention on the bandage and smiled when she saw it was still dry. It must have been awkward for him to clean around.

He dragged his hands through his wet hair as he walked towards her. "That feels much better."

She stood, careful not to meet his gaze in case he saw the desire swimming in her eyes. "I'll be right back." She headed for the kitchen to wash her hands and gather the medical kit.

When she returned, she worked silently, concentrating only on cleaning and re-dressing the wound. She was happy with the stitches and as she finished taping the bandage down, she told him so.

"Just another scar to add to the collection." He pushed to sitting in front of her when she was done.

"How many scars do you have?" she asked curiously.

He twisted so she could see his back. Various raised

lines crisscrossed his skin. Although they looked faded with age, she cringed. "How did you get these?"

He moved back to face her. "Farm accidents and sporting injuries mostly. My dad had even more." His eyes glossed over then.

"Your dad?" she asked. "He's passed on, hasn't he?"

Lachie nodded. "That's right. More than ten years now."

"I'm sorry for your loss." She brushed her hand over his before quickly drawing back. Then, Abbie stood. "I need to do some jobs and get some groceries. Will you be okay by yourself?"

He waved the *Outback* magazine at her. "I'll be fine, thanks."

"Is there anything you want from town?" she asked as she gathered her keys and bag.

He looked at her and a mischievous smile creased his face. "Could you get me some Coke and maybe a bag of chips?"

She smiled. "Sure. What flavour chips?"

"Salt and vinegar."

Her own mouth started watering as she imagined the tangy taste. Personally, she preferred lightly salted. "You're as bad as Hannah; she loves them too." Abbie opened the door. "I'll buy enough for both of you. She'll never forgive me otherwise."

"Thanks, Mum," he said in a sing-song voice just as she closed the door behind her.

She loved taking care of people; it was why she had become a nurse. Lachie was just another patient. She had to keep reminding herself of this.

Although she wouldn't mind if he were something more.

~

The supermarket was quiet today and Abbie enjoyed her solitude as she collected the products on her list. She paused in the snack section before selecting four large bags of salt and vinegar chips then made her way to the checkout.

She exchanged niceties with the woman working the cash register as she loaded up her purchases.

The bell above the entry door chimed, and Abbie looked up to see Maddie enter the store. "Hello, fancy seeing you here."

Maddie smiled and hugged her friend. "How is Lachie? I heard he's staying with you."

Abbie nodded. "He's good. He ended up having to have emergency surgery. The doctor wanted him to stay in town in case there were any complications."

Maddie smiled listening to the explanation but Abbie could swear she saw a shadow of emotion cross her friend's face. "Are you okay?"

Maddie waved her hand, dismissing her friend's concern. "I'm fine. Still recovering from the party."

"There were so many people. No wonder you're exhausted still." Abbie rubbed her arm. "It must have been great to catch up with everyone."

Maddie's voice softened. "Yes, it was a lovely day. It meant a lot to Dylan and me that everyone came."

Abbie knew Dylan was struggling emotionally. He had

a lot on his shoulders these days. A young family, that huge mortgage, and a drought with no end in sight. She might be new to the country life, but the plight of graziers had been in the news for several years now.

"Remember I'm here if you or Dylan need to talk," she said. "Or if you need anything at all. We love you guys." Abbie gave her friend a hug, which she hoped conveyed all the love she felt for her. When they parted, Abbie was sure she saw tears in Maddie's eyes.

"Thank you," she said. "That means a lot."

Maddie left to gather her own shopping, and Abbie paid for her groceries and returned to her car.

She wished there was more she could do for them. Not just Dylan and Maddie, but everyone who was struggling in the district.

She closed the boot of her car and looked around the main street. It was quiet even for a weekday morning. Across the road was the Banjo Patterson water feature and the tiny museum at the visitor information centre that Hannah loved so much.

Beyond that, she could just make out the roof of the community library. On a whim, she decided to drop by and see if she could find something for her houseguest to read. If he didn't have activities to do, she was afraid he might wallow in self-despair, especially being so newly sober. That certainly wouldn't help the healing process at all. No, what he needed was something to keep him entertained while he recovered at her house, especially when she was at work and not able to keep an eye on him.

CHAPTER 5

*L*achie wasn't used to being fussed over by women. His mother, who was a loving and caring parent, was being even more attentive.

"Mum, I'm fine," he said. "Abbie's taking good care of me."

Harriet gave him a stern expression before handing over his laptop. "Okay, you can work on this, but you better be sure to rest too."

Lachie took the computer before she could change her mind. There always seemed to be emails to reply to and work to be done. Sometimes he felt like he spent more time in his office than on the land itself.

"Thank you. Now I won't be stressing so much." He shot his mother a smile and placed the laptop on the coffee table beside him.

He didn't mind being laid up so much when Abbie and Hannah were around, but without them, the house was quiet and lonely. Lachie banished a tug of loneliness.

Outside, he heard the hum of an engine. Abbie was home.

Forgetting his injury, Lachie leapt from his chair and hurried out to help her.

"You shouldn't be lifting heavy bags," Abbie said, stopping him when he reached for a green canvas bag.

"Then give me the light ones," he insisted.

She pointed to the smaller of the shopping bags, and he lifted them with ease. "Mum's here."

"Oh, good. I was worried you'd be lonely."

The strength of the sun slanting through the oversized window bathed the kitchen in warmth. Lachie went to work putting the shopping away, shooing Abbie when she tried to help. "I can do this," he said.

Abbie sat with his mother and the two women chatted on like the best of friends. Harriet asked after Hannah and from the way she spoke, Lachie could tell she yearned for grandchildren. His thoughts turned to Darcy and Meghan, and he wondered what their journey to parenthood held. It must be hard wanting something so much but having it just beyond reach.

Harriet stayed for lunch and before any of them knew it, Hannah came bounding in, schoolbag flailing and long blonde hair whipping her flustered face.

"Hannah, this is Lachie's mother, Harriet." Abbie introduced them as she collected her daughter's discarded belongings.

"Hello." Hannah smiled and waved at Harriet before sitting next to Lachie and turning her attention to him. "Guess what I can do?"

He leaned toward Hannah. "What?"

"I can curl my tongue." She opened her mouth and curled up the sides of her tongue to form a tube shape.

"Hey, look at that." He smiled back at her. "Guess what? I can do it too."

Hannah's mouth dropped open as she watched him demonstrate.

"My teacher said it's something not everyone can do." She turned to Harriet. "Can you do it?"

With a wink, Harriet curled her own tongue. "Both Lachie's brothers can do it as well."

Hannah's mouth was wide open and her eyebrows high. "Mum, can you do it?"

Abbie squirmed slightly in her seat. Not obviously, but Lachie could see it. She seemed to concentrate hard on manoeuvring her tongue into the position but just couldn't do it.

"My teacher said that most people can't." Hannah explained. "It's hereditary, so my father must be able to do it."

There was an awkward silence for a moment before Abbie stood. "You must be hungry." She walked swiftly into the kitchen and busied herself preparing afternoon tea.

"I'll help." Lachie followed while Hannah turned her attention on Harriet and started explaining everything else she had learnt that day at school.

"You okay?" Lachie asked Abbie quietly when he was sure Hannah wasn't listening.

Abbie nodded but concentrated hard on cutting up the apple in front of her. "She doesn't mention her father. I mean, we don't talk about him."

The hair on the back of his neck rose. "Did he hurt you?"

"No, nothing like that." She looked over at Hannah, still deep in conversation. "She's never met him. He doesn't even know about her."

"Oh," he said, not sure what to make of the situation. He knew Abbie must have a good reason for doing what she did, but the idea of not being told you were a father just seemed wrong to him.

She sighed. "I'm sorry. Let's not talk about this." She put the apple in a bowl and took it to the table.

He leaned back against the kitchen bench and watched as Hannah sat down and munched on her fruit. If he were her father, he'd want to know about her. Hell, he'd want to be in her life. This man, whoever he was, didn't know what he was missing out on. Poor guy.

Abbie was paler now. Whatever had happened must have been big. Abbie wasn't the sort of woman to lie or deceive anybody. Then again, maybe that was why she had taken a job in the middle of nowhere. Maybe she was running from her past. From him.

A surge of protectiveness overwhelmed Lachlan. He couldn't let anything happen to these two. If they needed his protection, then he would keep them safe. Whatever the cost.

∼

After a delicious reheated meal courtesy of Harriet—chicken pie tonight—Hannah was ready for bed. She tugged on Lachie's hand and pulled him into her room.

"These two please." She handed over the picture books she had selected for him to read.

He sat next to her, on top of her pink doona cover, and she snuggled in beside him. When she nudged at his arm, Lachie draped it around her shoulder, before opening the first book and starting to read. She stopped him every now and again to point out a feature of the picture or ask him to explain a word. The more he read, the more comfortable he felt and the more animated his performance became.

When he closed the last book, he felt a tinge of disappointment that she didn't beg for more. Instead her eyes were starting to droop and she opened her mouth in a yawn.

"Good night, squirt."

She held out her arms for a hug and he obliged. He breathed in her fresh soapy smell and wondered at the tightness of her arms around his neck. Was this what it felt like to be loved unquestioningly?

When she finally let go, he climbed off the bed and caught Abbie watching them. She walked past him and bent to kiss her daughter good night. He left the room, giving the family some privacy.

Pausing in the living room to gather the library book Abbie had brought home for him, he brushed his fingers over the hard cover. The picture of an old farm house spiked his curiosity.

He had never been much of a reader. Having been forced to read the classics at boarding school always seemed more like a punishment than a way to escape the troubles of the real world.

Lachie read the back cover description again. It promised to be an outback murder mystery story.

"I can take it back if you're not interested."

He turned in surprise to find Abbie standing right behind him.

"No, it sounds good." He shot her a smile of gratitude. "Thanks."

"No problem." She moved into the kitchen and flicked on the kettle. "Would you like some tea?" Hair had escaped her ponytail and fallen across her cheek. He curled his fingers into a fist to stop himself reaching out and tucking the silken strands behind her ear.

"No, thanks. I think I'll have an early night." He watched as relief flickered over her face.

"Good. You should be resting," she said. "Do you need anything?"

He shook his head. "See you in the morning." He walked past her and headed to bed. He needed to sleep and regain his composure.

The prudent action would be to leave before he became any more involved with Abbie and Hannah. To hell with what the doctor said—he'd be just fine at Brigadier Station.

But the thought of leaving them now tore at his heart. He liked it here with them. He enjoyed their company and easy banter.

He enjoyed being the man he was when around them. Maybe he was growing up, away from the carefree, spur-of-the moment man he used to be when drinking and flirting had been second nature to him. That man was gone, and he could see now why he couldn't have remained living that lifestyle. He had never meant to hurt anyone, but he had never thought about the consequences of his actions.

As he slipped into Abbie's bed, he reminded himself of the pain he'd caused his mother and brothers over the years. The worry and disappointment he'd often seen in their eyes.

He never wanted to see it again. And he never wanted to be the one to cause it in Hannah or Abbie's eyes either.

~

Work and her regular routine kept Abbie busy the next few days. Lachie continued to spend mornings and evenings with them, but as soon as Hannah went to bed he would disappear to his room. As a nurse, Abbie was pleased he was resting so much, but as a woman, she missed his company. There was just a new intensity in his gaze when Lachie looked at her, and a constant vigilance when they were in close contact.

Well, he wouldn't have to avoid her company much longer. Tonight would be his last night in her house. Tomorrow he would go home and they could both resume their normal lives.

With the dishes cleaned up and Hannah asleep, Abbie was surprised that Lachie was still up, stretched out on the couch.

"Not having another early night?" she asked.

He turned his attention from the television. "Nah, I finished the book this afternoon." He pointed to the novel she'd borrowed for him. "I'll drop it off tomorrow on my way home."

Abbie walked over and sat opposite him. "Did you enjoy it? I thought I might read it after you."

He nodded. "It was good. I think you'd like it too."

Abbie fought to keep her attention on his face and not on the curl of his bicep as he rubbed his chin. "How about we watch a movie?" she said. "That is, if you're not watching anything on TV?"

His eyes widened. "I haven't watched a movie in a long time. I'd like that."

"Really? I guess I'll let you choose one then," she said before listing all the movies she had on DVD or could stream. "We also have every Disney movie ever made."

Lachie chuckled and the sound of his laughter warmed her from the inside out.

They settled on a blockbuster and after starting it, Abbie sat at a safe distance next to him on the couch, the last bag of salt and vinegar chips between them.

She wasn't taking any chances on chemistry blind-siding her. Thanks to the volatility of her emotions, she was already far too aware of the cowboy beside her.

～

Lachie awoke later, the movie having finished and the night still dark. He stretched his stiff neck, his gaze catching the top of Abbie's blonde head resting against his chest. Her hand was warm against the top of his thigh.

He liked the way it felt, her weight resting against him. The smell of her hair, so close and inviting. He carefully brushed a pale blond strand from her cheek. Below his fingers, her skin was soft and warm. Attraction kicked deep within him. Since he'd arrived, he'd struggled to repress the realisation he'd never met a woman quite like Abbie. But it didn't matter how much she affected him or how much he was drawn to her. Their timing couldn't be worse. Besides, he would never be worthy of Abigail Forsyth and her daughter.

She stirred and rubbed her face against his chest, sending his blood south. It was a good thing he was leaving in the morning. Keeping his distance from Abbie was proving harder every minute he was around her.

She rubbed her eyes and stretched away from him.

"We missed the end of the movie." He spoke with what he hoped passed as a casual tone.

She stared at the TV screen, still dazed with sleepy confusion. "I must have fallen asleep. Did you too?"

He nodded and stretched has arms out in front of him.

"I should go to bed." She pushed herself up from the couch, putting a safe distance between them. "I have work tomorrow."

"Yeah, me too. Big day." He stood and walked to the kitchen where he poured himself a glass of water. "Thank you for letting me stay here this week."

She placed a mug in the sink next to him. "No problem. I'm glad you're feeling better but remember, only light duties for the next few days."

"I will." He lost the battle to look away from the soft sweep of her bottom lip. Silence shrouded them. His heartbeat thundered in his chest. Then he leaned close and kissed her on the cheek. He didn't even realise he was doing it until his lips were on her soft skin.

He heard her draw in a shaky breath.

"Night," he said and moved past her, then he paused, wondering if he should apologise. When he turned his head to look at her, she had raised her hand to her cheek, to the spot where moments before his lips had been.

He turned and forced himself to walk away before she spotted him. And before he did something really stupid.

∼

Abbie waited until she heard the bedroom door close then collapsed onto the nearest chair. Feelings and sensations she hadn't felt in such a long, long time were now brimming at the surface. When he'd kissed her cheek, all she'd wanted to do was move her head and taste him right back.

She had been fighting this attraction since she had first met him; now all she wanted was to give into it.

But she couldn't. She lived in a small town. Small enough that people knew each other's business, and as a nurse she needed to be respected. The last thing she needed was patients talking about her behind her back. And they would talk. Lachie was a big enough figure around town to be of interest to all the town gossips.

Earlier, at work, a woman had come in with a suspected broken arm. While Abbie was assisting the doctor, the patient had asked how Lachie was doing. It seemed everyone knew he had been injured and that he was staying with her. Stunned, Abbie had brushed it off, simply saying he was recovering well and would be back to his usual self soon enough.

Abbie never should have offered her home to him. It was unprofessional. And dangerous. He could have been a thief or a drug dealer for all she knew.

He was a recovering alcoholic, after all.

But she had trusted her gut and now she was really in trouble. The handsome grazier from Brigadier Station might not have stolen anything from her, but she knew she could too easily give him her heart if she wasn't careful to protect it.

She turned off the lights, brushed her teeth, and climbed into the spare bed beside Hannah. She needed to sleep; she had a long shift ahead of her. But she knew Lachie would fill her thoughts again tonight and that tomorrow, when he was gone, she would feel his absence keenly.

CHAPTER 6

*A*fter an expectedly restless night, Abbie got up and dressed in her uniform. She attached her pendant watch to her shirt and tied her hair back before waking Hannah.

Her daughter rubbed sleep from her eyes as she climbed out of bed and yawned. "Is Lachie really leaving today?"

Abbie looked up from tying her shoelaces. "Yes, he's got a lot of work he needs to do on his farm."

"They're not called farms, Mum. They're called cattle stations." Her daughter said matter-of-factly.

Abbie smiled. "You're right, of course." She stood and assessed herself in the mirror.

"Do you think we can visit Lachie? At his station?"

Abbie looked at Hannah's reflection in the wall-length mirror. "Would you like to do that?"

Hannah nodded. "It's really big, and they have lots of animals. They used to have horses too, but his brother took them when he moved. I'd like to go horse riding one day."

"Well today you need to go to school, so get up and get ready." Abbie made a shooing motion before leaving the room and heading to the kitchen. She could smell tea brewing.

Lachie was already awake and dressed in those just-tight-enough jeans and a red-checked work shirt. She swallowed hard and tried to still her thumping heart.

He smiled at her. "Good morning. I made you a cuppa."

She watched as he added milk to her mug and ignored the pang of pleasure that he knew how she liked her tea. "Thanks."

She busied herself making two bowls of cereal and trying not to get too close to the hunk of a man taking up most of the space in the tiny kitchen.

"Darcy has to pick up some supplies today, so he's going to pick me up around ten," Lachlan said as he settled into a chair at the dining table. "Okay if I stay until then?"

"Of course," she said. "Now, remember what I said about rest. You don't want to get another hernia."

He quirked an eyebrow. "I could put up with any injury, so long as you were my nurse." The sound of his low, deep voice curled through her.

She swallowed but her mouth was dry.

She concentrated on making breakfast, but she could feel Lachie's gaze on her. It was unnerving and exciting at the same time.

Hannah skipped into the room, always so full of energy and excitement.

"Can you teach me how to ride a horse?" she asked Lachie as she climbed into his lap.

He wrapped an arm around her middle so she wouldn't fall off him. "I'm not the horseman of the family. But Darcy could. He breeds them out at Arabella Station."

Her eyes widened. "Why don't you ride?"

He shrugged. "Horses just aren't my thing. I like motorbikes."

"Harriet said you had an accident on a bike. Maybe you should ride horses instead," Hannah said.

"You know you can have accidents on horses too?"

Hannah just shrugged off his comment.

Abbie put her cereal on the table and Hannah moved off Lachie to eat.

"Would you like to come visit the station? Most of our cattle are away where there is better grass and we don't have horses, but you know what we do have?" Lachie asked.

Hannah looked up. "Dust?"

Abbie laughed alongside Lachie.

"Yes, there's lots of dust, just like at Maddie and Dylan's because they're our neighbours. But we also have chooks."

"Are they friendly? Can I pat them?" she asked in between mouthfuls.

"Yes, you can pat them and cuddle them." He smiled.

Hannah looked at her mother. "When can we go there?"

Abbie couldn't disappoint her daughter when she was so excited. And she would be able to check in on Lachie, make sure he was following her instructions. "How about next weekend? I have Sunday off."

Lachie caught her gaze and nodded. "It's a date."

CHAPTER 7

"Come on, Mum." Hannah poked her head out the car's window as Abbie stood outside the house, trying to think if she had everything she needed for their adventure to Brigadier Station. Hannah had been up early, so excited to see Lachie again and his famous property.

After pulling the door shut behind her and locking it, Abbie walked down the path and climbed into the driver's seat.

She twisted to check on her daughter. "Do you have your seatbelt on?"

"Yep. Let's go." Hannah clapped her hands together.

Abbie started the car and took a deep breath. This was probably not such a good idea. It had only been a few days since Lachie had gone home but the house felt so empty without him. That first night back in her own bed had been hard. She had come home exhausted from a busy day at work and hadn't bothered changing the sheets. His strong masculine scent had filled her dreams and by the time she had woken up, she had been hot and needy. Just thinking about him while she touched herself had made her come within seconds.

Changing the sheets hadn't been enough though. His spirit seemed to linger in her kitchen and living room. She expected to see him walk in the door at any moment and ask if she needed a hand.

It didn't help that Hannah kept talking about him and asking when they would see him next, like he was a part of the family. Abbie hoped that today would show him in a different light and that the man he had been with them was just one side of Lachlan McGuire. At home, in his own surroundings, he might be someone quite different.

The countryside all looked the same out here: long, dusty paddocks with minimal amount of livestock. The odd kangaroo or emu picked at a tussock.

Abbie had driven this way a few times before when visiting Maddie and Dylan. As they passed the driveway of their friends' house, Abbie stared down the long dirt road and wondered what Maddie would say if she knew Abbie spent her nights fantasising about Lachie McGuire.

Abbie and Hannah continued down the road another few minutes before reaching the sign welcoming them to Brigadier Station. Her stomach flip-flopped knowing that within minutes, she would see him again. Hannah started chatting loudly, her excitement rising the closer they got.

Finally, the modest, white homestead appeared and Abbie pulled up out front. The door to the house opened and Harriet and Lachie came spilling out. Hannah was out of the car and running to them before Abbie had even unclicked her seatbelt.

"Hi." Abbie waved as she emerged from the car. Lachie

was kneeling in front of Hannah, deep in quiet conversation.

Hannah was so attached to him. This could only end in disaster.

After a warm embrace, Harriet took Abbie's hand and led her inside. "How about some smoko? I've made Anzac biscuits."

The smell of baked goods filled the house, and Abbie's stomach rumbled just thinking about it. The two women chatted while they drank tea and waited for Lachie to come in with Hannah. When he finally did, the little girl's cheeks were pink and there was dirt on her shirt.

"I want a chicken," she announced as she pulled on her mother's sleeve. "They have six hens and one rooster and there are eggs that will hatch into chicks, and Lachie said we could have one."

"I said if your mum agreed you could have one." Lachie picked up a biscuit before sitting in the vacant seat next to Abbie.

Hannah turned pleading eyes on her mother. "Can we? Please?"

"I'll think about it." Abbie used her go-to response.

"Let's wash your hands," Harriet said, directing Hannah to the hall. "Do you like lemonade or juice?"

Abbie smiled at their retreating backs, then turned to Lachie. "She's been talking about you ever since you left."

Lachie's gaze was surprised but thrilled. "Has she?"

Abbie nodded and hid behind her cup. "Have you been resting?"

"I have. You can ask Mum if you don't believe me."

She put on her most crisp, professional voice to hide the thundering of her heart. "And how's the pain?"

He shrugged. "Getting used to it."

She wanted to ask him if she could take a look at the wound. To reassure herself he was healing and not just telling her what she wanted to hear. But she didn't trust herself to touch him. Not when the images of his shirtless torso were still so vivid in her mind.

She swallowed. "When's your follow-up appointment?"

His blue eyes fixed on hers. "In two weeks."

She nodded, caught in his stare. "I'll make sure I'm rostered on then."

∼

He had missed her. Lachie had tried not to think about Abbie Forsyth since he had returned home. When he hadn't been working on the computer, he had been reading a novel Darcy had lent him. The love story in it had particularly struck a chord. The hero didn't believe he was worth loving until the right woman came along and loved him for the man he was, warts and all. It had made Lachie wonder, hope really, that maybe Abbie would do the same for him. If she was willing, that was.

Hannah was as bright and bubbly as always. He had certainly missed her cuddles and sweet words. Being with them had shown Lachie what he was missing. He was in his mid-thirties, all his friends had settled down, and he was still single. Was that really the life he wanted?

Could he find someone who would love him despite

his history and all his bad decisions? Could that person be Abbie?

Hannah made herself the centre of attention and Harriet gushed over her. She had so much love and affection to give the young girl, and Hannah seemed to enjoy their time together as much as Harriet. Lachie laughed at Hannah's jokes and, when she came over and perched on his knee, he bounced her gently, enjoying her closeness.

He observed Abbie from the corner of his eye. She was ever watchful, making sure her child was safe and enjoying herself. Lachie could only imagine what it must be like to be solely responsible for a whole human being. To know that their entire happiness depended on the choices you made and your actions.

Moving to the outback could have been a terrible mistake, but instead, Hannah was thriving, learning and discovering new things, like how to pick up a chicken.

"Has Darcy left then?" Abbie asked.

Lachie nodded. "He and Meghan had an appointment to get to in Townsville so they flew out yesterday.

Harriet collected the empty mugs. "It was just like old times having him here. But he couldn't wait to get back to his wife."

Lachie rarely envied either of his brothers. They were both happy living their lives with the women they loved and doing jobs they enjoyed. But over the last few days, when Darcy spoke about Meghan, or when Lachie heard them speak on the phone, Lachie was reminded that they had something he didn't. The love of a good woman. Someone to share everything with. The good and the bad times. He realised now that he'd always held a part of himself back, even when he'd been engaged to Meghan. He'd never found a woman who made his breath falter or made him want to risk everything for.

He'd never realised how much he wanted that.

He stole a glance at Abbie. She was exactly the kind of woman he liked—long, wheat-blonde hair, full, luscious lips, and eyes that saw into your soul.

Hannah leaned back against Lachie's chest and looked up at him with her big round eyes. "Could you show us around the station?"

"Are you sure? There's nothing much to see except dirt, dust, and broken fences." He shrugged.

"I wanna see where you grew up," Hannah insisted.

Lachie glanced at his watch. "Okay, we could have a quick tour."

Abbie stopped him before he stood up. "We wanted to drop by and see Maddie and Dylan on our way back. Are you sure there's time? I don't want to interrupt them while she's making dinner."

"There's still plenty of time," Lachie said. "Like I said, there's not much to see."

∼

"Is this why I got the front seat?" Abbie asked as she clipped her seatbelt back in. "So I can open and close all the gates?"

Lachie sent her a heart-melting smile. "There are only a couple more."

In the back seat, Harriet was pointing out various

birds and landmarks to Hannah who seemed totally engrossed by the tour.

"Do you own all of this or do you share it with your brother?" Abbie asked.

"Brothers—I have two. Darcy you know, and Noah is working in WA with his girlfriend, Riley," Lachie explained as they bounced over a pothole. "But to answer your question, yes, I own it. I inherited it when our father died over ten years ago now."

"What's it like? Being in charge of all this?"

"Well, there's always something to do and always bloody bills to pay." He shifted the gear and his hand bumped her leg.

"Ten years, huh? Isn't that about as long as this drought's been going?"

He nodded. "Drought's been going a bit longer actually. We did get a little bit of rain a couple of years back, but not enough to make a difference."

Abbie smiled and tried to imagine this landscape in shades of green and cream instead of the browns it was now. "What was it like before the drought?"

He caught her eye and held her gaze for a moment before turning back to the road ahead. "The pastures were full of beautiful fat Droughtmaster cattle and we had frogs." He smiled. "They would croak so loud we couldn't sleep. Now, it's quiet. So very quiet."

Abbie watched him as he gazed longingly ahead. "I hope the rain comes soon. I'd like to see that."

"See what?" Her daughter chirped up from the back seat.

Abbie turned to look at her. "We were talking about

frogs."

"Where?" Hannah moved closer to the window and studied the landscape.

"You won't see any out there, squirt," Lachie said. "When it starts raining, that's when they'll come back."

They continued their short tour to the windmill, then to the paddock by the river where a handful of creamy cows were dozing under the shade of some gum trees.

"Those are the only ones left here," Lachie explained as they watched from the vehicle. "All the others are on agistment down south."

They watched as some cockatoos flew between the branches above the cattle, then Lachie put the Land Cruiser back into gear.

"We should head back if we're going to see Dylan and Maddie before it gets too late." Abbie said.

She let her mind wander as they drove the short distance back to the house. Could she see herself living out here? So far removed from town? It had the potential for being devastatingly lonely. Not for strong, hardy women like Harriet and Maddie though. Those women seemed made for country living.

It couldn't be that bad. Could it?

From the way Hannah chatted, she would be very happy to move out here this very moment. She had already named the chickens and was trying to convince Lachie to get her a poddy calf next breeding season.

Lachie parked the car and everyone got out. After collecting her bag and keys, Abbie said her goodbyes to Harriet.

"You two are welcome here anytime. It's been such a pleasure having you."

"Thank you for having us. It's been lovely." Abbie hugged Harriet before turning to Lachie.

"Would you mind if I came with you?" he asked. "To Dylan's? I haven't heard from him since the party."

Abbie nodded. "Of course. Did you want to drive with us?"

"No, I'll follow in my ute."

"Can I go with Lachie?" Hannah turned to her. "Please?"

Abbie knelt down to her daughter's level and spoke softly. "He doesn't have a car seat and it's only a short drive to Maddie's."

Hannah's shoulders slumped but she didn't argue. Instead, she climbed into her seat and waited patiently.

The convoy pulled up at the neighbouring homestead a while later. Maddie came out and hugged them in greeting. "To what do I owe this visit?"

Abbie smiled and nodded at Lachie who was being led away by Hannah and Jamie.

"We were visiting Lachie so thought we'd drop by."

"Were you now?" She quirked an eyebrow. "Is something going on between you two?"

Abbie looked away from her perceptive friend. "No, of course not. Just checking in on a patient."

Maddie put an arm around her shoulder. "I like Lachie. He's a nice guy, but he has a past." Her tone was serious and tender. "He used to be quite the womaniser. And drinker. Most nights of the week he was at the pub, so just be careful. I don't want to see you or Hannah get hurt."

Abbie nodded. She knew Lachie's reputation before he had sobered up, but that wasn't the man she knew. That was the old Lachie. He hadn't even made a pass at her and the little flirting he'd done had been in good humour.

Unless he wasn't interested in her. Maybe he simply wasn't attracted to her after all.

Then Lachie was beside her, shaking hands with Maddie. "Where's Dylan?"

Maddie's face glazed over with concern. "He went out a few hours ago." She looked at her watch. "He should've come home by now actually."

Abbie swallowed and caught Lachie's eye. Dylan wasn't in the best mental state these days, and Maddie had confided in her that they were on the brink of bankruptcy.

"Is he alone?" Lachie asked and pulled out his phone.

Maddie nodded and the women waited while Lachie called his neighbour.

He shook his head. "Voicemail. Did he take the radio?"

Maddie nodded, but when they tried that there was still no answer. Abbie had to push down the rising panic in the pit of her stomach. "Why don't Lachie and I go and look for him? Can Hannah stay here with you?"

Maddie's lip quivered. "We had an argument. I told him I had applied for a job. Telemarketing I could do from home." Abbie hugged her friend as her voice hitched. "What if he's done something stupid?"

"I'm sure he's fine," Lachie said, climbing back in his ute. "Stay close to your phone."

Abbie gave her a squeeze before following Lachie to his vehicle. "It'll be okay," she called as they drove away.

Lachie handed her his phone. "Call Mum and ask her to come over straight away. I have a bad feeling about this."

Abbie did as he asked without question.

She had the same bad feeling.

CHAPTER 8

*T*he engine hummed and the ute bumped over the sun-hardened ground. Neither of them spoke. Abbie prepared herself for the worst. She had learnt to listen to her gut, and all signs were pointing to there being something terribly wrong.

Dylan hadn't answered his phone or radio. That meant he couldn't reach it. Even with spotty reception, Lachie had assured her phones would work anywhere out here.

Farm accidents were a common cause of injury in the outback and the cause of most of the emergencies she dealt with at the hospital. Vehicle rollovers, electrocution, and drowning were all possibilities.

But given Dylan's state of mind and the fact he had argued with Maddie, Abbie was worried it was something else. Either he had disappeared or worse.

Lachie straightened in his seat, and she felt the tension transmit from his body. She turned and looked in the direction he was staring.

The fading sun glimmered off the top of Dylan's red ute like a beacon drawing them in.

Abbie gulped as Lachie sped towards the vehicle. She studied the scene as it came into view. Lying on the ground were a pair of denim clad legs and workboots; the rest of the body was hidden behind his vehicle.

No sooner had the car rolled to a stop than she was throwing open the door and running over. Her sandals filled with the gritty dirt as she ran and she inhaled the dry air, thick with the stench of death.

She froze. Vomit filled her mouth.

Birds. Pieces of skull. And blood.

Oh, so much blood.

Lachie moved and shielded her view of the scene with his body.

She stared at the buttons on his shirt and focused on her breath. She would never be able to forget what she had just seen. It would be stored away with the other victims and patients she had lost.

She had never seen anything like this before though. Never known the victim before.

"I have to check for a pulse," she said, more to herself than him.

He turned and looked over his shoulder briefly. "I don't think that's necessary."

Their eyes met in shared pain and anguish. "I have to help if I can. You need to call triple zero."

He held her gaze for a moment as though assessing if he could possibly talk her out of it. Then he nodded and pulled out his phone.

She listened to him explain the situation as she walked slowly to the body.

The rifle he had used lay on the ground to his right.

She waved her hands and shooed the pair of crows who were feasting on the meat from the hole in the back of Dylan's head.

He was dead. She knew it before she pressed her fingers to his neck and felt nothing but cold, hard flesh.

Dylan Sears, husband, father, and friend, had taken his own life.

The smell of bodily fluids and blood finally got the better of her, and she stumbled to her knees then crawled away from the body before heaving up her stomach.

Lachie pulled back her hair and gently rubbed her back. "The police and ambulance are on their way." His voice helped to calm her from the panic she felt rising. "There's nothing we can do. Or could have done."

Tears blurred her vision. She wiped her mouth then turned into his open embrace, wanting, needing his comfort and assurance.

"I didn't think he would do it. I thought he was over the worst part." She hiccupped.

"Me neither." He stroked her hair, and she felt a warm wetness drop onto her forehead.

Abbie wrapped her arms around his back, and they held each other tightly as their sobs joined together as they mourned the loss of their friend. She had the feeling that this would irrevocably change them.

Both separately and together.

～

"Did you find him?" Maddie's voice was full of hope at the other end of the phone, and Abbie steeled herself to deliver the news.

"Is Harriet there yet?" Abbie asked. Maddie would need someone there with her.

"Yes. Abbie, tell me."

Abbie closed her eyes, hoping for the blank darkness they offered, but instead she saw Dylan's mutilated head and the glassy, faraway look in his eyes. "I'm sorry. There was nothing we could do."

There was a thump on the line as though the phone had been dropped, then all Abbie could hear was her friend's wailing cries and Harriet's soothing voice. She hung up and said a silent prayer, hoping she could send her love and strength to her.

Lachie had found a blue tarp in his ute and had covered the body.

The crows were finally gone, but the stench remained.

"Have some water," Lachie said and handed her a bottle. She took it from him and drank deeply. Her throat was dry and scratchy from her earlier despair.

"How long do you think they'll take?" she asked, referring to the emergency services.

"Maybe another half hour. Did you check on Hannah?" He stood next to her, leaning against the ute as the sun descended.

"I didn't get a chance." She hoped her daughter would never have to witness something like this or go through what Maddie was going through. Abbie gazed out at the flat landscape and setting sun. "It will be dark soon."

He nodded. "I'll turn the ute's lights on when it's too

dark to see." He gestured to the spotlights that were rigged up on his vehicle.

He put his arm around her shoulders and held her against his side. Abbie closed her eyes and leaned against his shoulder. Exhaustion settled in her bones, and she tried not to think of all the what-ifs that played on her mind. What if they had arrived earlier? How could she have helped Dylan more?

"I think he held out for the party," Lachie said quietly. "We had a chat that day. I thought he was just being friendly, but now that I think about it, he was saying goodbye."

Abbie pressed her face against his chest and breathed him in, focusing on his musky scent so she wouldn't cry. "It will be terrible for Maddie. And her children. Their dad is gone."

Lachie wrapped his arms around her and held her tight. His body was reassuringly strong and stopped her from falling apart again.

His lips brushed the top of her head. It felt so nice. So comforting. She wanted more.

She raised her head to look at him. His eyes were glassy as he gazed back at her. He lowered his head and she pressed her lips against his. The instant her lips parted beneath his, it was as though she went into a freefall. Rationality, logic, caution all ceased to exist. There was only the two of them. The man who bewitched her senses and filled the empty part of her. He tightened his arms around her and she lost herself in his musky scent and skilled mouth.

Eventually, when her mouth was suitably swollen, he

pulled his head back and looked into the distance. "They're on their way. I can hear the sirens."

Abbie opened her eyes to the darkness that now surrounded them. "You should turn those lights on then," she murmured and made to leave his embrace, but he pulled her closer. "Just one more minute."

In unspoken agreement, she relaxed back into him and snuggled her face into his neck.

This was where she wanted to be right now—safe in their bubble. The world didn't really exist. It was all a dream.

She breathed in deeply. Lachie's smell was still strong, but there was another scent fighting to be noticed. It was enough to yank her back to reality. She moved her hands to his chest. "They'll be here soon."

This time, he let her go. She took two steps away, cold now that she wasn't cocooned in his warmth.

He opened the ute door and started the engine. Bright light illuminated the paddock. "I'm going to drive around to the other side so they can see him better," he called from the cab.

Abbie nodded and folded her arms around herself. She wasn't sure if she was shivering from cold or shock. The night was warm so she suspected the latter.

Lachie parked the vehicle in the new position and left it running. He climbed out and leaned against it. As though drawn to a flame, Abbie couldn't stay away. She walked over and stood close by, but dared not touch him.

"About before …" She started.

Lachie put his hand up to stop her. "We can forget it happened. If that's what you want."

She couldn't see him clearly but she knew he was looking at her. "I, ah …" She didn't know what to say. Did she want to forget about kissing him when it had been so amazing?

Light bounced over the landscape as vehicles approached them, their sirens turned off.

"Let's talk about it some other time," he said before pushing off the ute and walking to meet the police car.

She watched his silhouette as he stepped into the path of light. Even if they pretended their kisses hadn't happened, she knew she would never forget them.

It was the single good thing to have come out of this terrible experience.

～

Lachie shook the police officer's hand and headed back to his ute. He closed the door quietly behind him, trying not to wake Abbie who had retreated there a while ago after answering everyone's questions.

She didn't stir when he reversed the ute and drove back to Maddie's house.

What a day. It had been filled with highs and lows. Kissing Abbie was definitely a high, but he would have preferred their first kiss to have happened under better circumstances.

He pushed away the thoughts and visions that threatened and concentrated on driving. Kangaroos would be out now, and the last thing he needed was to hit one.

Abbie finally woke just as they were pulling up in front of his house.

"Why are we here?" she asked groggily.

Lachie turned to her. "Mum brought Hannah over. She's asleep inside."

"Oh, good." She rubbed her eyes. "I'll get her and take her home."

"It's after midnight. Why don't you sleep here tonight and go home tomorrow?"

She studied her watch before nodding. "If I leave early enough, I can still get Hannah to school and go to work."

Lachie considered suggesting they all take the day off. Now wasn't the time to discuss it. Better to wait and see how they felt in the morning.

Lachie walked ahead and waited for her at the door. He let her step through in front of him where she was greeted by Harriet.

"Come with me, love. I'll show you where you can sleep." His mother took her by the arm and led her down the hall.

Lachie turned to the kitchen and opened the fridge. Damn, he needed a drink. A stiff whiskey would be perfect right now. Instead, he reached for a can of Coke. After popping the lid he took a long gulp, ignoring the bubbles and fizz that tried to escape. He walked out onto the verandah and perched himself on a chair. Darkness loomed heavily, and he let it surround him.

"You'll be up all night now," his mother said and walked past him. She must have turned a light on. He hadn't noticed.

"Huh?"

"The caffeine will keep you awake."

"I'm not sure I want to sleep tonight anyway," he admitted, sure if he closed his eyes he would see Dylan.

"Well, it'll have to be on the couch if you do. Hannah is in the spare bed and Abbie's in yours. Hope you don't mind."

He shook his head, then suddenly remembered how messy he had left his room that morning.

"It's okay. I picked up the dirty laundry before you got here."

"Thanks." He tried to smile at her. But it felt wrong. How could he smile when his neighbour was dead? "He was my age. He had a family."

Harriet placed her hand on his knee. "No one ever knows what truly goes on inside another person's mind. He chose to do this, and we all need to find a way to live with it."

"It's just such a waste."

"It is."

They sat in silent vigil for some time. Lachie thought back on memories with Dylan. They hadn't been the best of friends, but they had been there for each other when they'd needed help with a fence or other farm issue.

Noah and Dylan had been good mates. His brother had spent a lot of time at his neighbours' place last year when Riley had been helping Dylan out on the station.

"I'll call Noah in the morning and let him know. Darcy too." Lachie said.

"Yes, there are a lot of people who will need to be contacted. Maddie will need to organise a funeral too, poor thing."

"She's not alone, is she?"

Harriet shook her head. "I called in the CWA and they were going to take shifts looking after the kids. Margaret was there when I left."

"Good." The Country Women's Association could always be counted on in times of need, especially when something like this happened. Dylan's suicide certainly wasn't the first the community had suffered nor was it likely to be the last, unfortunately.

"If it's okay with you, I'm going to lie down," Harriet said.

"Of course. Go to bed." He stood and hugged his mother. The urge to make sure everyone around him knew how much he appreciated them was strong. "I love you, Mum."

She squeezed him back. "I love you too, darling. Wake me up if you need anything or want to talk."

"Thanks."

When she had left, he sat back in the chair and closed his eyes. Instead of Dylan filling his thoughts, it was Abbie. He let himself remember every detail of her. The faint floral scent of her perfume. The sweet eagerness of her lips, and the pliancy of her body.

She was everything he would ever want or need in his life, and he resolved to be the kind of man she would consider falling in love with. To have her and Hannah in his life would be more than he had ever hoped for.

He would make sure they never had to go through something like this again. He would protect them from all evils life threw their way. If he had them around, he would never leave them.

~

Abbie woke to a damp pillowcase. Rolling onto her back, she stared at the ceiling, hoping it had all been a dream. A really bad, vivid, dream.

She turned her head to the window. Early morning sun snuck under the curtains.

She focused her thoughts on those little things. The light. The quiet house. The smell of the sheets. It was such a comfortable bed. Softer than the one provided for her at the house in town. She rolled onto her stomach and ran her hands over the mattress. She could feel Lachie's impression. She inhaled deeply and closed her eyes, letting herself imagine him there, with her. What would it be like to wake up next to him?

She opened her eyes with a start. She couldn't let herself go there. Now was not the time. She had to get up and drive Hannah back into town. She had school, and Abbie had work today.

She threw back the sheets and dressed in yesterday's clothes. No one else was up in the house so she padded lightly along the hallway. After visiting the bathroom, she headed for the living areas. She poured herself a glass of water and stepped out onto the veranda into the cool morning. She leaned against a post and took in the scene in front of her. Light burst across the sky in brilliant swathes of gold, orange, and pink as the sun grew larger.

A banging noise shattered the silence of the morning, and she turned in its direction.

She followed the well-worn path, past some cattle yards and an assortment of other farm buildings, until she reached a corrugated shed. The hammering continued, echoing out of the building. She peeked her head in. As she'd suspected, Lachie sat at a work bench tinkering with pieces of machinery.

She cleared her throat before speaking. "Morning."

He turned to her. The circles under his eyes told her he hadn't slept. "Morning. How are you?"

She shrugged and walked farther into the shed. A bright fluorescent light hung above her, casting shadows into the corners of the room. "Thanks for giving up your bed."

"I owed you for letting me have yours." He attempted a smile but it fell flat.

"I just wanted to say thanks. I had better get Hannah home." She turned to leave.

"Wait." Lachie rose from his chair and slowly walked towards her.

His five o'clock shadow made him even more swoon-worthy. A mixture of wood, leather, and something she couldn't quite pinpoint caressed her sense of smell, making her feel a little light-headed. She licked her lips, her mouth suddenly dry. She gulped, her heart thudding crazily as he came closer.

He reached out a hand and grazed it over the hair at the side of her face then lower, down her throat and across her shoulder. His calloused fingers gently scraped her tender skin. He didn't say anything, just stared deeply into her eyes.

She wanted to kiss away their pain, just like they had yesterday.

Instead, he withdrew from her and plunged his hands into the pockets of his jeans. "Drive safe."

She nodded and took a step backwards. "Thanks."

Abbie looked back at him from the door. He had returned to his work, but was still watching her.

She raised her hand in a wave before walking outside and treading back up the path to the house.

It had seemed like he'd wanted to say something to her, but held back at the last minute. She wondered what.

It was probably for the best.

She reminded herself of all the reasons that they shouldn't be together. His history as a flirt and woman-iser. She couldn't risk her heart on a man with that kind of a past. She couldn't risk Hannah's either. Her little girl was already so attached to Lachie; she would be devastated if anything happened.

Then there was the fact he was a recovering alcoholic. He might be okay now, but she knew the slightest trigger could make him fall of the wagon.

He was too much of a risk.

She had never been one for gambling, and she wasn't about to start now.

CHAPTER 9

*L*achie mingled with the rest of the gathering crowd outside the funeral parlour. Solemn-faced mourners spoke in hushed voices around him.

Beside him, Darcy had his arm around his wife's back, and she dabbed at her eyes with a tissue. She looked tired and had barely stopped crying since arriving yesterday. Last night, Darcy had confided that she was on hormonal medication and had been feeling its effects for a while now. They had postponed their fertility treatment in Townsville to attend the funeral and spend some time with their friends and family, all of whom were feeling Dylan's loss deeply.

Lachie turned to see Maddie as she hugged his brother Noah and then greeted Riley. Riley had briefly worked for Dylan and had been the first to point out his failing mental health.

If only they could have helped him more. Even with all the programs the government and community created and all the counselling he had received, it still hadn't been enough.

Noah and Riley finished giving their condolences and walked over to stand with their family. Lachie shook his brother's hand. "It's good to see you again."

Noah nodded. "You too."

They had recently reconciled their differences. Their father's abuse had been uncovered and a deeper bond had been forged between them. It had also been the turning point for Lachie and the reason he had started his journey to sobriety.

"We should find our seats," Harriet said. "It'll start soon."

Lachie looked around the room, searching for one particular person with long blonde hair. He hadn't spoken to her since that morning. Many times he had picked up his mobile, wanting to hear her voice, but had never gone through with it.

He had hoped she would come today though. He wanted to see her, even if only for a moment and from a distance.

Then, as if conjured by his thoughts, she appeared in the doorway. Their gazes caught and held. He smiled for the first time in days.

"Whose that?" Noah asked, following his gaze.

"That's Abbie Forsyth, the new nurse." Harriet's voice was filled with friendliness and something else—hope?

Abbie was dressed in a simple, deep blue dress. Lachie drank in her curves and long, bare legs as she strode over. She was such a sight for sore eyes.

"Hi," she said, stopping in front of him.

"Hi Abbie." He wanted to kiss her or at least hug her, but with his family watching on and the service about to start, it didn't feel right. Instead he turned and introduced his brothers and their partners.

"Nice to see you again." Darcy shook her hand. "Will you sit with us?"

Abbie looked around as people started finding their seats. "Yes, thank you."

Lachie sat beside her on a plastic chair. Everyone who had attended Dylan's party and more were here today.

The party. Had it only been a few weeks ago? At least Dylan had seen everyone that last time.

Lachie wondered again if Dylan had planned it so.

The service started and the congregation fell to a hush as stories were told and memories shared.

"I'd like to invite Abigail Forsyth up," the minister said.

Lachie turned to Abbie with a frown.

She gave him a nervous smile before standing and walking to the stage.

After picking up a microphone, piano music filtered through the speakers in the ceiling and Abbie opened her mouth and started singing.

Lachie sat in stunned silence as her melodious voice filled the room. As she sang the familiar tune about being comforted by angels, he was filled with the deepest sensation that he had heard her sing before. He caught the memory and studied it, trying to place where and when he had heard her before.

She struck a particularly high note and he felt the

rapture of the crowd around him. All were awestruck in her presence.

Applause broke out as the final notes of the song faded. She thanked the crowd before handing the microphone back and returning to her seat.

"That was amazing," Lachie whispered and reached for her hand.

She smiled at him and entwined her fingers with his.

They sat like that for the rest of the service, though he didn't know what else was said or done. He was too focused on the frissons of energy sparking from their joined hands.

At the end of the service, people stood and greeted their neighbours. Lachie reluctantly let go of her so she could be commended on her performance.

"Is that Paige and Logan?" Noah asked, pointing to a couple on the other side of the room.

Lachie recognised his old school friend. He looked the same despite being ten years older now. "I wonder how they knew Dylan."

They followed the crowd as it moved outside for refreshments and fellowship. With Abbie busy with her new fan club, Lachie directed his attention to greeting his old friend.

"G'day Logan." Lachie shook his friend's hand

Logan grinned back. "It's been too long." Then he turned to the attractive brunette beside him. "This is my wife, Paige."

Lachie released Logan's hand and shook the woman's slender one. "Nice to meet you. I heard you remarried."

Logan looked at him sheepishly. "I couldn't resist falling in love with the help." He turned adoring eyes on his wife and she blushed.

"I was his kids' governess," she said.

Lachie grinned. "So you knew all his bad habits going into this. Smart."

"*My* bad habits?" Logan punched his friend playfully in the arm. "I was never as bad as you."

Lachie shook his head. "No, you weren't, that's for sure." He found Abbie in the crowd and felt his pulse quicken. "But those days are behind me now. I've cleaned up and am focusing on the future and keeping the station afloat."

"Good on you," Logan said, his voice softer. "Terrible situation, this. We've lost a lot of good graziers to suicide."

"Yes, too many," Paige agreed.

Lachie nodded and scraped his hand over his freshly shaven chin. "How did you know Dylan?"

"I know Maddie through School of the Air," Paige explained. The online teaching school was used for most children in remote and regional areas of Australia.

"Of course." Lachie nodded. "For a big country, it's a small world."

Logan smiled.

Abbie had finally made her way through the crowd and hugged Paige and Logan in turn.

They chatted on as the crowds slowly dissipated. Noah and Riley, and Darcy and Meghan joined them, and the young people discussed the drought, beef prices, and other rural issues.

After promising to visit Brigadier Station the following day, Logan and Paige headed off.

"I better go. Hannah will be finishing school soon," Abbie said.

"I'll walk you to your car." Lachie placed his arm around her back, feeling the warmth from her body under his palm.

"This is going to sound strange," he said when they were alone, "but I've heard you sing before."

She stopped walking and turned wide eyes on him. "You can't have. I hardly ever sing in public."

"All I can remember is it being a hot and dusty afternoon with lots of people around. You were singing a song. I can't remember what but I remember your voice." He gave her a sheepish look. "It's unforgettable."

That gorgeous pink stained her cheeks. "I haven't spent much time in the outback and that was the first time singing in …" she bit her lip as she thought, "… about seven years."

"You never came out here before now? Or somewhere dry and dusty? How about a B&S ball?" he said, referring to the frequent bachelor and spinster balls popular with young, single country folk.

He caught a look of recognition cross her face before she looked away and started walking again.

"The only other time I've visited the outback was when I went to the Birdsville Races, but that was years ago."

"That must be it. I used to go all the time." He smiled, finally having cracked the mystery of where he knew her from. "I can't remember many specifics but I'm sure that's where I would have met you."

She shot him a smile which didn't reach her eyes.

She unlocked her car and looked up at him. "Thanks for walking me out."

"It was good to see you." The urge to kiss her was strong, but he held back. She had a sudden standoffishness about her. Like she would bolt if he tried anything.

He opened the door and held it open. "I'll see you later."

She nodded and climbed in.

He watched as she drove away, still wondering what he had said to make her suddenly so wary.

∼

"He was at the races the same year as me," Abbie said in hushed tones over a wine that evening.

Paige and Logan were staying at the hotel up the road, and Paige had come over at her friend's desperate pleading.

"Okay." Her friend urged her on.

Abbie chewed her lip as she considered her words. She had never told anyone this before, but she knew she could trust Paige with the story. She wouldn't even tell her husband.

"I went to Birdsville Races seven years ago. A bunch of friends, other nurses, wanted to blow off some steam, so I tagged along. I didn't really want to go, but I needed a break from work, study, and my parents."

"So you went to the races?"

Abbie nodded. "I really let loose, like, completely out of character. I got really drunk and did stuff I wouldn't normally do." She thought back on the snippets of things she remembered from that weekend. The taste of dust in her mouth; the camels, and the smell of beer and bourbon. "I slept with a guy and nine months later ..."

Paige's eyes widened. "Wow, I thought Hannah's father was an ex. I didn't realise it was a, what, one-night stand?"

Abbie nodded. "I don't remember anything about him. His name, what he looked like-anything."

"You weren't drugged, were you?"

"No, my friend, Jo remembers a bit. She said I was acting really happy and buzzed, but I definitely didn't take anything."

"Okay. So you were drunk and slept with someone willingly and got pregnant."

Abbie nodded.

"And now you think Lachie was there."

"He remembers me singing. Jo said I jumped up onstage and sang some country song. I kind of remember seeing this big crowd cheering me on."

"Wow, what are the chances?" Paige leaned back in her chair as she let the information sink in.

"Yes. What are the chances ...?"

Paige turned to her abruptly, and goosebumps rose on Abbie's skin. "What are the chances Lachie's the guy you slept with?"

She nodded. "He was drunk too, and he has a reputation of sleeping around."

"Hannah does have the same blue eyes as him."

"They can both roll their tongues and I can't."

Silence descended as Abbie considered the possibility. "He is familiar," she said. "When we kissed, it felt familiar."

"Wait. You kissed?"

Abbie explained how they had found Dylan.

"Oh, wow. That must have been so traumatic." Paige rubbed her arms.

"It was. But, Lachie was there and we shared the grief together. He comforted me. I don't know how I would have coped without him."

"Are you in love with him?"

Abbie's head shot up. "No. I mean, I like him. But, no, I can't go there. He's got a past."

"We all have pasts, Abbie. You have a baby from a stranger you can't remember."

Abbie shrugged. "You're right, but what if he relapses?"

"He's come so far. Logan told me what he used to be like, and I can't even believe he's the same guy. Maybe he's worth taking a chance on."

"Maybe."

"Do you know his blood type?"

Abbie shook her head. "You think I should see if it's the same as Hannah's."

"You know more about it than me, but isn't that a step you can take before doing a paternity test?" Paige asked.

"Yes. There's only a couple of blood types that would match." She considered the consequences of finding out. "His blood type will be in his records at the hospital."

"Then you need to find out. One step at a time."

"Should I tell him?"

"No. Find out for sure before dropping this on him."

Abbie swallowed the last mouthful of wine from her glass.

What if it turned out Lachie was Hannah's father? Would that be a bad thing, really? At least the mystery would finally be solved, and Hannah would have a dad.

But was Lachie ready for that responsibility? And was Abbie ready to be tied to him for the rest of her life?

CHAPTER 10

"Why did you go into nursing when you could have become a famous singer?" Logan asked Abbie late the following afternoon as they sat around a campfire.

Abbie laughed. She had never considered music as a serious career. She had enjoyed studying it at school, but nursing was her calling. "My parents would have disowned me," she said and smiled at her friends. Hannah was at Lachie's side, slowly turning a sausage speared on a stick over the edges of the fire. Lachie was close enough and keeping an eagle eye on her so she wouldn't hurt herself.

She trusted him with her daughter. She had never trusted anyone other than her parents and close friends. But she knew without a doubt that Lachie would protect Hannah and look after her.

And she adored him back. He was the only father figure in her life. Possibly more than just a figure given what she had found out.

"How are your kids, Logan? Still riding those horses you got them?" Darcy asked from across the firepit.

"They sure are. I started something there; they're all horse mad now. Especially Scotty."

"Horses are great with autistic kids though. Do you think it's helped?"

"Sure has. You should see them together."

Darcy was obviously horse mad himself. Meghan had explained how they lived on a station a couple of hours away called Arabella Plains, and as well as running beef cattle, they bred campdrafting and stock horses.

Darcy reached over and squeezed Meghan's hand. "We've been talking about learning more and doing some study. We'd like to open a camp or something like that for kids with learning disabilities."

"We have such sweet animals," Meghan explained. "They would be perfect for kids with autism."

"That would be fantastic," Paige said. "We'd love to help."

Abbie felt at ease around these good, country folk. It warmed her heart to see that the younger generations were continuing their parents' community spirit and pride in the land. They could have moved to cities and towns and gotten easier jobs with higher rates of pay, but instead they had chosen to stay on the land and help support their rural communities. Abbie couldn't help but respect them for that.

She turned to Riley who was sitting on her left and the only member of Lachie's family she hadn't spoken to at length yet. "I heard you and Noah are based in Western Australia. What are you doing there?"

Riley swept her long dark locks over her shoulder. "I'm a helicopter mustering pilot so we're following the work and exploring the countryside. Have you ever been west?"

Abbie shook her head. "I'm a city girl; this is as far west as I've ever been."

"If you get a chance you should come visit. Perth is a great place-not that I'm a fan of big cities and crowds of people." Riley struck Abbie as a woman full of guts and determination, used to living in a man's world and able to give as good as she got.

"I'd love to see it one day. All of the outback seems so foreign. It's like being on Mars."

"It is," Riley agreed. "You should see it from the sky. So vast and undisturbed."

The women continued chatting until Paige tapped her on the shoulder. "Help me get the salads?"

They linked arms and walked into the empty house.

"Did you find out his blood type?" Paige asked eagerly.

"Yes. I checked this morning at work." Abbie looked around to make sure there were no listening ears. "He's a match."

"Wow." The word escaped her friend's mouth.

"I have a friend in Brisbane who could do a DNA test. I just need to get a sample from Lachie."

"What kind of sample?"

"Some hair or fingernail clippings. Or a swab from his mouth, but that might be a bit obvious."

"So sneak into his room and find something. There must be some hair on his brush."

They arrived in the kitchen, and Paige pointed her down the hallway. "Do you know which room is his?"

Abbie nodded.

"Then go. I'll keep watch."

With a pounding heart, Abbie crept down the hallway and turned into Lachie's room. She saw the bed and remembered how soft and inviting it was. Again, she wondered what it would be like to lie in it with its owner. She shook her head and focused on her mission. On top of the chest of drawers was a mirror and bingo, a brush.

She pulled out a clean tissue from her pocket—she was always prepared for snotty noses—and used it to pull some brown strands from the brush.

"Meat should be ready soon." Lachie's voice loomed from the living room.

Abbie pocketed the tissue and ran from the room and collided straight into a hard chest. She gulped as she raised her head.

Lachie looked at her with a tilt to his head. His strong jawline was thick with stubble, adding to his rugged appeal. "Were you in my room?"

"What? No." She stepped around him. "I was in the bathroom." Blood pounded in her ears, loud, intense, as though in warning. Everything tightened, from the tiniest muscle in her body to the very air surrounding them, as if the world held its breath, expectant.

He nodded slowly at her. "Why are you being so weird around me?" He lowered his voice. "Is it because we kissed?"

That was as good a reason as any. "Yeah, I'm sorry. I guess I'm embarrassed."

His laid his hands on her shoulders. "You don't have to be. Not with me." The raw, intense emotion in his voice touched her even more than his husky words. Their gazes remained locked. A gaze of yearning, of need, of hope. The need to kiss him, to taste him again almost overwhelmed her.

But he might be Hannah's father and until she knew for sure, she couldn't do anything.

"I should get back to the kitchen and help Paige." She slipped out of his grip and turned from him.

The sooner she had the results, the better. This was torturing her.

∼

When the food was dished up, Lachie studied Abbie. Her pale hair was pulled back into a ponytail to reveal the smooth pale skin of her nape. He ground his teeth. He could memorise every delicate contour and satin-soft curve, and still he'd never be able to get enough of her.

He wanted to ask her how she was coping. If she often woke in a cold sweat too. When a rush of grief and anxiety engulfed her, if her knees went weak. It seemed no matter how hard he pushed his emotions into the depths of his subconscious, they continued to crawl to the surface, and all when he least expected it. So often since the accident he had found himself gasping for air, thankful no one was around to watch as his emotions and fears threatened to tear open his soul.

"What do you think Maddie will do now?" Harriet asked the group, pulling him from his reverie.

"Sell the station probably," he said before taking a bite of sausage. As much as it pained him to lose his neighbour, he didn't think she'd have much choice.

"I don't suppose you can buy it?" Noah asked.

Lachie shook his head. "As much as I'd like to, there's no way a bank would give me a loan right now. We're stretched enough."

"I heard the Hendersons sold their place to overseas investors," Meghan said. "Such a shame to be losing a family with such a long history on the land."

"The Hendersons? They were one of the first settlers. They used to breed merino sheep way back in the day." Lachie remembered the stories he had learnt from his school history lessons.

"Things are changing," Harriet said. "We just have to make the best of it."

The sombre mood once again descended over the group.

"Little Jamie was well-behaved at the funeral," Abbie said.

Lachie glanced at his sister-in-law. He had spotted her looking longingly at Maddie's son. She had always had a soft spot for the little boy. His heart tightened in his chest and he sent a hope into the universe that Meghan and Darcy would soon be blessed with a child of their own.

"Yes he was." Harriet voice was filled with emotion. "Poor thing, losing his father so young."

"I really liked the photo collage they played," Riley said. "Does anyone know who organised it?"

"I did," Abbie said quietly from her spot next to Harriet.

Eyes turned in her direction.

"I planned most of it with the funeral director. Maddie wasn't up to it."

"It was beautiful." Harriet placed her hand on Abbie's. Lachie wished he was sitting there so he could touch Abbie's hand as well.

He missed touching her.

And kissing her.

Hannah left her spot on the ground and walked over to Lachie before flinging her arms around his neck. Her skin was soft against his rough cheek.

"Hello, squirt." He stroked her hair. "Have you had enough to eat?"

"I feel sick."

He watched as she held her stomach. "Did you eat too many sausages?"

She nodded and stuck out her bottom lip.

He wrapped his arms around her, holding her against his chest and rocking her gently, side to side.

From across the fire, Darcy cleared his throat and Lachie looked up to see everyone staring at him. They all looked surprised, even amused.

Abbie was almost pale in the firelight and Lachie wondered if she was feeling sick too.

"Wow, I didn't know you were so paternal these days," Noah said beside him.

Abbie stood and walked around. Bending down, she put her arms out. "I can take her."

"She's okay," he said earnestly.

Abbie shook her head. "It's getting late. We should go home."

"I wanna stay here," Hannah complained.

"Just a few more minutes." Lachie didn't know why Abbie was behaving like this. He could feel everyone watching them.

Her voice was quiet but demanding. "She's *my* daughter. Give her back."

Lachie let go of Hannah and put up a hand in surrender. "Come on, squirt. Time to go home."

"No," she said as Lachie stood her up. Abbie grabbed her daughter's hand and pulled her away from him.

Abbie rushed her goodbyes, loaded her daughter into the car, and was gone before Lachie got a chance to get over the shock of what had just happened.

"What was that all about?" Darcy asked him as the car lights disappeared down the driveway.

"I have no idea," he admitted. "She's been acting weird lately, but never like that with Hannah."

Darcy looked at his wife, chatting with Riley. "Maybe she's jealous. She's had Hannah to herself all this time, and now she's getting attached to you."

Lachie nodded. "That could be it."

Though he sensed something more. Especially after finding her in his room earlier.

What was that woman up to?

CHAPTER 11

*a*bbie stepped out of the air-conditioned confines of the hospital and took a deep breath of fresh, country air. The evenings were cooler now, and she had decided to walk the short distance home from work.

She turned down the street and was just passing the church when she heard her name being called.

She couldn't avoid him like she had so many times in the weeks since the funeral. He was walking towards her and he looked determined.

"Hi, Lachie." She kept her tone light and friendly, despite the pounding in her heart.

He came to stand in front of her. The faint scent of his aftershave swirled alluringly around him. She had tried so hard to forget the way he smelled, the way his blue eyes captivated her, and the way he kissed her.

She missed his kisses and his comfort. The last three weeks had seemed like an eternity.

"How have you been?" He shoved his hands in the

pockets of his blue jeans, and her gaze inadvertently followed the action.

She jerked her head away, coming to look just over his shoulder. "Fine, thanks." She lied. "You?"

He shrugged. "Alright."

She made the mistake of catching his eye. There was so much left unspoken between then.

And the one big secret Abbie was holding onto.

She looked around the church yard, grasping for a neutral topic of conversation. "What are you doing here?"

He breathed out the initials. "AA."

"Oh."

He scratched his neck. "I've been attending more regularly since, you know, Dylan."

"That's great. Of course this must be such a trying time." With everything going on, she hadn't even thought about how Lachie would be handling things. Not just the loss of his friend, but the trauma of having found him.

"The hospital has a good counsellor. I've been seeing her." Her boss hadn't given her much of a choice in the matter. Couldn't have a nurse break down in theatre, after all.

"I know. She called me and we talked."

It surprised her to hear that Lachie had opened up to someone. She had expected him to be like other men and bottle up all his feelings. Like Dylan had at the end.

"And you haven't been drinking?" she asked.

He shook his head. "I wanted to, that's for sure. But these meetings have helped. And work." He laughed his deep, throaty laugh. "You should see Brigadier Station. It's never looked cleaner."

She smiled at him. "I'm so happy for you."

He reached out his hand to hers, and their fingers linked. It was a brief moment, but long enough for her heart to ache. She could feel his body heat drawing her in. Her mouth went dry. When she looked up, he caught her glance and held it with those amazing blue eyes of his. The corners of his mouth curved just a little, causing tingles to course through her body.

She dropped her hand and crossed her arms. "I've got to go."

She turned to leave.

"I miss you."

She started at his softly spoken words. Vulnerability covered his face.

She swallowed hard. "I can't do this."

"Why not?"

The words were on the tip of her tongue. But once she spoke them, she knew she would never be able to stop the tornado of events that would follow.

"I just can't," she said before turning and walking away from him as fast as she could.

~

"Thanks for helping out. I don't know what I would have done without you," Maddie said with a worn smile.

Lachie tilted his head before lifting the ute's tailgate back into place and locking it securely. "I'll come back after the rodeo and start on the bore pump."

Maddie shaded her eyes from the sun. Gauntness hollowed her face, and dark circles stained the spots under her eyes. These past few weeks had taken their toll on Maddie Seares, and Lachie wished he could do more to help.

The whole community had gotten behind Maddie and her kids. The CWA were over every day with food and would clean and babysit while Maddie and Lachie maintained the station.

A large "for sale" sign had been erected, but so far there had been no bites. There wasn't much demand for a de-stocked cattle station when the future of beef was so uncertain and the drought so damaging.

"I still can't believe there's going to be a rodeo in our honour," Maddie said.

"Believe it. Ticket sales have gone through the roof." Lachie had joined the committee formed to plan the event. All the proceeds would be given to Maddie to help tide her over for a while. She had confided to Lachie that the bank was threatening to foreclose and she had no idea where to get the next payment from.

She threw him a tight smile. "And with Darcy competing and Riley running helicopter flights it's become a family affair for the McGuires."

Lachie put his arm around Maddie. "You're family to us. We'll do anything we can."

Her face clenched and her eyes overflowed with tears. He pulled her in for a hug.

"I'm sorry," she said when she pulled away, wiping her eyes with her shirtsleeves. "I never thought I'd be here. A widow with two kids in charge of a cattle station."

"You've been dealt some tough cards." His heart ached

for her. What a shitty situation she was in. "Surely it can only get better."

She sniffed and looked up at him. "Jamie is looking forward to the rodeo. He wants to try the mechanical bull."

"Uh-oh." Lachie laughed. "Maybe we can get him to stay on the safer rides that won't encourage a career as a bull rider. I hear there will be a Ferris wheel."

"Yes, that would be much better."

Lachie waved a goodbye before climbing into his ute and heading for home.

The last few weeks had been busy, but lonely. After the funeral, his brothers and their partners had gone home and the house had once again fallen quiet. His mum was always good company, he couldn't ask for a better mother and housemate, but he missed the noises and companionship of other people.

He missed Hannah's enthusiasm and zest for life.

He missed her mother too.

He hadn't seen or heard from Abbie since that day in the church parking lot. He had tried to find out what was going on with her, with them, but she had clammed up again, leaving him with the belief that she didn't want him after all. Those kisses had just been a result of their shared experience and nothing more. He had obviously misread the affection in her eyes.

So he had focused on other things. Helping Maddie on her property and planning the rodeo had taken up all his spare time.

Now, on the eve of the big event, he knew he would be returning home to a houseful of visitors. He had seen

Riley and Noah fly over in their Robinson R44 a few hours ago on the way to the landing strip on Brigadier Station.

Darcy and Meghan had horses to float over from Arabella Plains so they would want to arrive before dark.

His thoughts travelled to Abbie again. He wondered if she would come to the rodeo. Hannah would surely want to go, and he doubted Abbie would deny her such an authentic outback experience.

He couldn't wait to see them. Even if it was just a passing glance.

If she didn't give him some reason to hope she still felt something for him, he would bury those feelings for good and forget about her.

This was his last chance.

CHAPTER 12

"Oh my God," Judith Forsyth said, clamping her hand over her nose. "That smell is disgusting."

Abbie took a deep breath and counted to five in her head. "It's a rodeo, Mother. There are lots of animals here."

Judith looked down at her leather sandals, which were now coated in sand, and Abbie suspected gritty particles were now rubbing the soles of her mother's feet. Well, that was one way of getting a foot scrub.

"You could have told me to bring boots," Judith said.

"You wanted to come to a rodeo. You should have known boots and jeans were the dress code," Abbie said, waving at her mother's cream linen shirt and black trousers.

At least her father looked more the part in his designer denim and polo shirt. He was in deep conversation with his granddaughter as they walked towards the entry of the arena.

Country music blared through the speakers, and food

smells lingered in the air. They showed their tickets and were ushered into the festivities just as the noise of a helicopter whooshed up in the distance.

"That's Riley." Hannah waved as the helicopter lifted up.

"Who?" Judith asked, her hand raised against the bright afternoon sun.

"One of our friends," Abbie said then steered the group down a long alleyway filled with food vendors and sideshow alley games.

Hannah pulled on her grandfather's arm and pointed to a ball-toss stand. "Can we play, please?"

"Sure," he said, easily giving into her whim.

That was what it had always been like with him. Adam had always showered his only grandchild with gifts, as if that could replace her not having a father. Hannah had become spoiled and selfish in Brisbane and Abbie had spent many months teaching her she couldn't always get what she wanted.

Abbie sighed. A few games and treats today would be fine. It was big gifts, like the expensive clothes her mother had brought with her when she'd arrived last week, that Abbie didn't appreciate. Especially when they were dresses and skirts entirely unsuitable for life in an outback town.

But while Hannah had received gifts, Abbie had received a talking down. "When are you going to be finished this crazy experiment and move back home?" Judith had said, waving her arms around the tiny house that all up was the size of their living room back in the city.

"We like it here," Abbie had said. "We have friends and I love my job."

"This is no place to raise my granddaughter. She needs to be around people of education and good breeding, not a bunch of cow farmers."

Abbie had scoffed. There were many types of education to be had, and her mother's idea of it wasn't necessarily the best. "They're graziers, Mum. They run cattle stations, not farms."

Judith waved her hand. "And I'm sure they do it very well, but do you really want to see Hannah live the rest of her life out here? Do you really want to settle down with a … grazier?"

Abbie paused. Did she? Could she?

All the while she had been contemplating her relationship with Lachie, she had never really paused to think about the long-term consequences.

He would never move to the city. His whole life was here. Even holidays away would be difficult to plan because there were animals to look after.

Her mother had looked at her then, hope in her eyes. "Abigail …" Her mother used that tone and her full name even though she knew Abbie hated it. "Have you met someone out here?"

Abbie had turned away so her mother wouldn't see the flush rising on her skin. Fortunately, Hannah had chosen that moment to steal Judith's attention and the subject hadn't been broached again.

"Oh, wow, that's Zoe Gilmore." The excitement in Hannah's voice made it rise even higher than its usual soprano tone.

"Who?" Judith asked, and everyone turned to where Hannah was pointing. A tall, slim woman with long, curly blonde hair stood at the side of the stage talking to a man whose back was to them.

"She's like this amazing country music singer." Hannah turned to Abbie. "Can we meet her?"

"I don't know if she's meeting people. She must be about to go onstage."

The man she was talking to turned and Abbie stilled. It had been far too long since she had seen that face.

"It's Lachie." Hannah squealed and started running towards him.

Abbie called her name but she kept barrelling along. The adults had no choice but to follow.

By the time Abbie and her parents reached them, Lachie had lifted Hannah onto his hip and she was talking to the singer.

"Would you and your dad like a picture?" Zoe asked.

"Yes," Hannah said

"I'm not her dad," Lachie said at the same time.

Abbie's heart squeezed. She stepped forward. "I'm sorry about this. She got away from us."

Zoe smiled at her and Abbie focused on the superstar in front of her, all done up in heavy makeup, a guitar slung over her shoulder. "You must be Hannah's mother." Zoe extended a hand, which Abbie shook. "I'm Zoe."

"Hi, I'm Abbie. We're big fans."

"Can we take a photo?" Hannah turned to her mother.

Abbie finally looked at her daughter, which also meant looking at Lachie since they were so close to each other.

He cleaned up nicely. Too nicely. She wondered if he'd

been making moves on Zoe before they'd come over. She couldn't remember if the star was single or not.

Lachie lowered Hannah to the ground.

"If it's okay with Zoe." She smiled and when Zoe agreed, Abbie fished out her phone.

"You have to be in it too, Mum."

Her father offered to take the photo, so she handed over her phone then stood beside Hannah.

"And Lachie too," Hannah said. "You need to be in the photo as well."

Abbie watched as Lachie raised his eyebrows questioningly. When Hannah waved him over again he relented and moved to stand beside Abbie. His arm brushed against her, and she tried hard to concentrate on smiling for the camera.

"Get in a little closer, Lachie," Adam said, gesturing with his hand as he studied the phone screen.

Lachie stepped in and snaked his hand around her waist. Even the simplest touch left her breathless with desire. Their gazes collided and his smile faded as his blue eyes gathered intensity.

When Adam finally lowered the camera, Abbie stepped out of his embrace and moved a safe distance away.

Hannah hugged Zoe. "Have a great show."

"Thank you. I hope you enjoy it." She kissed Hannah's cheek and smiled at the family.

Hannah moved to stand by her mother as they watched Zoe start up the stairs. Her name was announced and cheers went. There was no need to move from their practically backstage view.

"Hi." Lachie's voice was a whisper in her ear as he leaned in behind her. "It's good to see you."

She turned a fraction so he could hear her over the music. "You too. How are you?'

"Fine. You?"

"Good." Could this be any more uncomfortable?

Abbie remembered her manners then and turned to introduce him to her parents. Her father, Adam, took his hand and gave it a squeeze.

Judith looked him up and down speculatively. "Oh, so this is your grazier?"

Abbie swallowed and looked between Lachie and her parents. He frowned at her as thoughts raced through her mind. If she said yes, they would lay off her and stop asking when she was coming home. She would have a reason to be here. On a whim, she took his hand and nodded, hoping he would play along.

"Well, it's nice to meet you," Adam said, shaking Lachie's hand. "We've never met one of Abbie's boyfriends before."

Abbie wished she had put on more makeup. She was sure her face was tomato red now.

"She's quite a girl," Lachie said, squeezing her hand.

"Come and join us," Judith said. "We'd like to get to know you better."

Abbie looked towards her daughter who stood a few feet ahead, dancing to the music, none the wiser to the deceit her mother was acting out.

"I'm sure Lachie's really busy. He's on the planning committee."

"Are you?" Judith asked, looking, what was that? Impressed?

"That's why I was talking to Zoe. I organised for her to be here," Lachie explained.

"Well, she's a hit." Abbie waved at the crowd of people singing and dancing along to the performance.

"Shall we find somewhere and sit down?" Judith said.

"I'd love to join you, but I have to go and check on the rodeo guys. That part starts next." He looked straight at Abbie then. "I'll come back and find you in a while." He moved in and captured her mouth in a kiss.

It wasn't like before. This one was full of heat and desire. Like it had been building since the first day they'd met.

When he pulled away, Lachie flashed Abbie a look so raw and intense her breath caught.

Then he turned back to her parents and said his goodbyes.

Before leaving, he walked over to Hannah and whispered something in her ear. She laughed at whatever he'd said and hugged him.

Abbie wrapped her arms around herself and watched Lachie walk away. His promise to find her still rang in her ears.

That's what she was scared of. That when he found her again, this time, she wouldn't be able to let him go.

~

Lachie finished his to-do list in record time. Everything was going just to plan, minus a few small hiccups, which was to be expected. His duties to the committee were done until after the rodeo, so he set of in search of Abbie and her family. Their kiss still fresh on his lips.

People were packed in the circling grandstands like sardines and, around the far side of the arena, families and friends huddled on picnic blankets or in the backs of utes that had been parked there before sunrise. Everyone wanted the best spot to see all the action of the centre ring—the campdrafting, the barrel racing, and the bull riding.

Zoe Gilmore's unmistakable country twang sung the last strains of her most famous, award-winning ballad. The atmosphere was electric, the anticipation high as the crowd cheered loudly.

Lachie made his way through the crowds, scanning faces as he went, searching for Abbie.

He didn't know what was going on with her and her parents, but he wasn't one to look a gift horse in the mouth. If she wanted to shower him with affection and kisses, too right he was going to make the most of it.

Maybe this was just what they needed and while playing happy couples, he could show her how good they could be together and what she would be missing out on if she rejected him again.

He spotted Hannah first, jumping up and down and cheering as she watched the barrel racing start. A woman on a grey horse was first, the animal kicking up a plume of dust as she turned sharply around a barrel.

Taking the stairs two at a time, then shuffling his way past a row of people, Lachie finally reached the group.

"Lachie, here sit beside us." Judith shuffled over so he

could sit between her and Abbie. Hannah left her grandfather's side and perched herself on his lap when he was sitting.

"Hey squirt. Having fun?"

"Yes. Did you see the liberty horses perform to Zoe's song? They were dancing!"

He smiled at her enthusiasm. "It's cool, huh? It takes years of training to get a horse to do what you want like that."

"I wish I could have a horse." Her shoulders slumped. "Mum says I have to prove I'd be able to look after it. Are horses a lot of work?"

"They sure are. You have to ride them and wash them and feed them."

"But they eat grass. Why do you have to feed them?"

He smiled at her naivety. "Did you see any grass at Brigadier Station? Horses can't eat dirt."

A grin broke across her youthful face. "I could feed it apples and carrots."

He laughed. He'd missed their conversations. "Horses need a more substantial diet, hay and oats."

With the barrel racing finished, the campdrafting event was announced, and Darcy appeared in a slot.

"Isn't that your brother?" Abbie leaned over and asked, the smell of her floral perfume faint on her exposed skin.

Lachie nodded. He'd always been proud of his brother's achievements, even if he hadn't shown it. To a certain extent, he had been jealous. Darcy had been such a natural horseman. Lachie had never been really good at anything. Except drinking.

Abbie leaned forward, getting her parents' attention. "That's Darcy McGuire. Lachie's brother."

Her parents turned and they all watched intently as Darcy rode out on his black horse, Jasper. The smells, the dust, the cattle and horses, the cowboys, the cheering, and even the country music playing from the suspended speakers all combined to make his heart pump faster as Lachie watched his brother run the course. He was grateful to have something to focus on other than how good Abbie looked in her tight jeans and fitted blue shirt, and how her leg would bump against his from time to time.

Darcy cut the beast and easily sent him around the figure eight, finishing to a chorus of applause from the crowd. Their homegrown hero had done it again.

After the campdrafting was over, there was a break between events so the party decided to use the opportunity to visit some rides and get something to eat.

The lines for the food were long and filled with hungry children.

"We'll wait here and order," Judith said, motioning to a vendor selling burgers and other greasy delights. "You two go on some rides with Hannah."

Hannah took Lachie and Abbie's hands and tugged insistently, leading them in the direction of an ornate carousel. As beautiful as it was with its carved white horses, the line was short. Patrons preferred the scream-inducing adrenaline rides.

"Can I, Mummy?"

Lachie observed as Abbie smiled down on her daughter. "Okay. I'll watch from here."

When Hannah was safely aboard her pony, Abbie returned to Lachie's side. The cheerful music started and Hannah moved up and down and slowly around in wide circles.

"Sorry about before," Abbie said, her eyes still trained straight ahead.

"About pretending I'm your boyfriend?" Lachie smiled. "No problem."

She snuck him a glance. "My parents can be very … persuasive when it comes to where I live and if they think there is a good reason for me to stay here, they'll let up a bit."

Lachie leaned forward on the fence. "Am I a good reason to stay?"

She turned to look at him. "It's just pretend. Just for today."

He exhaled slowly and straightened. "There's no pretending on my part. I want to be with you, Abbie. You must know that. I want you and Hannah in my life." It felt good to say the words. To lay all his cards on the table.

She gaped back at him. "You do?"

He nodded and brushed his hand over her hair. It was just as soft as he remembered. She looked dazed, her skin flushed and her eyes half-closed. It was the sexiest thing he'd ever seen. "We could have this, you know. We could be a family."

Her eyes deepened and her mouth opened. He moved closer to her as her gaze slipped to his mouth. This was it; he would surely be able to persuade her with a kiss.

"There they are." Adam's brogue Scottish accent cut

through their tender moment like a knife. Abbie jumped out of his reach and backed steadily away.

Lachie turned to the older couple as disappointment curled through him. Turning on a smile, he gratefully accepted his food though he had no hunger for it anymore. He had an appetite for something else altogether.

CHAPTER 13

"Mum, look at me," Hannah called from the top of the sleek black horse, Jasper, which Darcy had ridden at the rodeo the day before.

Meghan, held the lead rope and led the giant of an animal around the yard in slow circles.

Abbie pulled out her phone and snapped some photos and video of her daughter with a big grin plastered on her face.

"She's a natural." Darcy spoke beside her. "Are you sure she's never ridden before?"

Abbie shook her head. "No, never."

She slid Darcy a sideways glance. He was so similar to his brother in appearance, she wondered if they were ever mistaken for twins. She hadn't seen Lachie yet today. Was he avoiding her on purpose?

Yesterday at the rodeo, Lachie had invited them out to the station so Hannah could ride Darcy's horse before they headed home to Arabella Plains. Adam and Judith had eagerly said yes and she guessed this was all part of their plan to size up their daughter's new boyfriend. Her parents were anxious for their daughter to settle down and marry. To give Hannah a permanent home with two stable parents. Did they still want that? Even if it meant she'd be living on a cattle station in outback Queensland.

"I haven't seen her this happy in a long time," Abbie said as her daughter pulled gently on the reins, turning Jasper around the corners.

Darcy leaned against the fence next to her. "She sure fits in well. Seems really fond of Lachie too. He's never spent much time around kids."

Abbie looked everywhere but at him, like an embarrassed child.

Her ride finished, Hannah climbed down from the horse and cuddled it around its neck before returning to Abbie. "That was awesome. I want a horse."

"Then you had better start saving for one."

They thanked Meghan and Darcy, who set about unsaddling the horse while Abbie and Hannah joined the rest of the party.

They found the group assembled on the verandah, sipping cold drinks and chatting. Judith and Harriet were sitting next to each other, deep in conversation, while Adam was holding court with Noah, Riley, and Lachie.

Abbie slowed as she took Lachie in. Tall, broad-shouldered and lean-hipped—by anyone's definition he would be considered gorgeous, especially with the tanned skin, and the angles and planes of his features. Not to mention those eyes.

As they got closer, he turned and their eyes met. "How was the ride?" he asked as Hannah skipped to his side.

"Amazing. Darcy said I'm a natural."

"Of course you are." He tickled her neck and she giggled.

Lachie's words echoed in Abbie's ears. *"We could be a family."* This strong and stoic cowboy was unlike any man she'd ever met. He wanted to be in their lives. Not many men would want to take on a single mother.

She stood next to him as he tickled Hannah. His five o'clock shadow made him even more swoon-worthy. A mixture of wood, leather, and something she couldn't quite pinpoint caressed her sense of smell, suddenly making her feel a little light-headed.

Shaking her head, Abbie walked over to the table and poured herself a glass of water, moving as far away from Lachie as she could. Riley pulled her into conversation and she found herself relaxing with her new friends.

"Lachie, do you have any tattoos?" Riley asked as Lachie moved to join the circle.

"Just the one on my back," he said, reaching behind him and pointing to the top of his spine.

Abbie couldn't help but remember the times she had seen him without his shirt on. She had never noticed a tattoo though. She wondered what it was.

"Abbie, do you have any?" Lachie's voice held a mischievous tone.

She shook her head. "No tattoo. I do have an ugly birthmark though."

"Noah wants something on his arm but he can't decide what," Riley said.

Noah strung his arm around her waist and pulled her

close. "Only if you get something too. I'd like a bird. Maybe an eagle."

Something tugged at Abbie's heart. No one had ever looked at her like Noah looked at Riley. She shifted her weight on her feet and became all too aware of Lachie standing right next to her. The heat of his body curled around her, making her blood sizzle with need.

Biting her lip, afraid of what she might say or do, she excused herself from the group and went inside to the kitchen where she found Meghan gathering her things. "The horses are all loaded so we'll be going as soon as we say goodbye."

"It was lovely to see you again." Abbie smiled, so grateful to have made friends with this kind-hearted woman.

"I hope you'll bring Hannah out to Arabella Plains sometime. We have plenty of spare beds," Meghan said. Abbie heard the sadness tinge her last remark.

"Thank you. We'd like that." Abbie looped her arms around Meghan in what she hoped was a supportive hug.

"And I'm rooting for you and Lachie. I can see how much he cares about you," Meghan said. "He certainly never looked at me the way he looks at you."

Abbie frowned. "What?"

"He would tell me he loved me, but I never really felt it." Meghan paused and studied her. "You know we were engaged, right?"

Abbie's mouth dropped and she felt the world spinning around her. "You and Lachie? Engaged?"

Meghan clamped her hand over her mouth. "I'm so

sorry; I thought you knew. Everyone knows, how do you not?"

Abbie backed away until she felt a chair behind her she could fall into. People had been eager to tell her about Lachie's drinking and womanising but no one had thought to tell her that he'd once been engaged? To Meghan? The woman his brother was now married to?

She couldn't bring herself to be upset with Meghan. Obviously she was deeply in love with Darcy now and happy in her marriage to him. But why hadn't Lachie told her? After all, he'd said he wanted her in his life, but had kept this crucial piece of information from her.

If he'd lied about that, what else had he lied about?

$\approx$

Lachie stood by the vehicles, waiting his turn to say goodbye to Abbie and her family.

"It was lovely to meet you, Lachlan," Judith said and pulled him down for a hug. "I can tell you have good intentions for our girls. Look after them for us?"

He kissed her cheek. "I will. You have a safe trip back to the city."

"I can't say I'll miss the flies." Adam moved forward and shook Lachie's hand. "Come visit us if you're ever in Brisbane."

Hannah threw her arms around Lachie and squeezed.

"Bye, squirt. You be good to your mother."

"Come see us soon?" she asked and Lachie looked up at Abbie. Any barriers he had pulled down were firmly back in place now. Something had changed and he was damned if he knew what.

"We'll see," Abbie said, directing her daughter to the car without so much as a wave to him.

Meghan tapped on his arm, and he turned in her direction. "She didn't know about us," she said as the engine fired and the car cruised away. "I thought she did so it kind of all came out. I'm so sorry."

Lachie rubbed his temple. It hadn't even occurred to him to tell her. They hadn't gotten to the point in their relationship where they discussed their exes. "It's not your fault. I wasn't keeping it secret; I just hadn't told her yet." He shrugged.

"She seemed really surprised and kind of devastated."

Devastated? That meant she really did feel something for him after all. Sure, he would have to work hard to mend what had broken between them, but at least now he knew it wasn't all in his imagination.

"Thanks for telling me."

"I really do hope it works out with her. You two would make a great couple." Meghan smiled. "And Hannah is just the cutest thing. If I didn't know better, I'd actually think she was yours."

He furrowed his brows. "What? Why would you think that?"

"Well, you obviously both adore each other, and she kind of looks like you. I mean she has the same eyes and even your noses are similar."

Lachie was speechless as he took in her words.

Meghan shook her head. "I'm on hormone drugs, so don't listen to me. I'm probably seeing things that aren't there." She turned and left Lachie frozen in place, mentally comparing images of Hannah with the vision he saw whenever he looked in the mirror.

No, it was just coincidence. Blue eyes—lots of people had blue eyes.

Besides, he'd never slept with Abbie so there was no way he was Hannah's father.

He scratched his head. It must just be a case of wishful thinking.

CHAPTER 14

*L*achie parked his ute in the hospital parking space and slammed the door behind him. It had been a week since Abbie had been at Brigadier Station, and she had been avoiding him ever since. She had ignored all his phone calls and texts. Even his bloody Facebook messages.

But today she was going to see him, even if he had to sit in the waiting room all day and night. Because this morning he had woken up with a memory of Abbie and her blasted birthmark.

He remembered tracing its oval outline. Kissing the soft skin where it lay, just below her left breast. He remembered kissing other parts of Abbie Forsyth too. Drunk or not, he remembered it all. Every touch, every kiss and every exquisite taste.

How could he have forgotten her, even for a moment? She had kissed him on a dare and he had thought he'd won the lottery. The most beautiful woman in the world had just flung herself in his arms. Of course he wasn't going to turn her down. He might have been a drunk, but he wasn't a complete idiot.

Kissing had led to touching, which had led to them ending up on the back of his ute with the full moon shining down on them.

He pushed open the doors to the hospital and stood in front of the empty reception desk. There was only one other person in the waiting room, a frail old lady he didn't know.

Ping. He tapped on the metal bell.

"I need to see Abbie Forsyth." He spoke as he spotted the receptionist peering out of a doorway. "It's an emergency."

She gave him a questioning look. "I'll see if she's free."

He paced circles in front of the desk while waiting for Abbie, all the time practicing what he would say to her.

"Lachie?"

He turned to see her walking towards him, dressed in her pale blue uniform, and his heart pounded.

"I remember." He strode towards her. "I remember Birdsville." He watched for a sign of understanding in her expression but she didn't even flinch.

"What are you talking about?"

He looked around to make sure there were no prying eyes or ears. "Birdsville. I remember that we spent the night together."

Her eyes widened and she inhaled.

"I remember your birthmark." He pointed to where he knew it was just under her chest. "It's oval and dark brown. Right on top of a rib."

She took a step back but remained silent.

"When is Hannah's birthday?" He had already done the calculations. Birdsville Races was an annual event in September. If Hannah was born in June, then he really could be her father.

Instead of answering though, Abbie put her hand up to stop him. "I'm at work; we can't talk about this here." Her tone was accusatory and her eyes warned him to stop pushing. "You need to leave me alone."

She turned on her heel and started walking quickly away.

He called after her but she just hastened her pace.

When she was out of sight, he smacked his palm against his forehead in frustration. Damn, now he'd pissed her off there was no telling what she'd do.

This was not how he'd planned it. He had thought, or at least hoped, that she would remember too and they could start planning their happily ever after. Now he was left with unanswered questions and suspicions.

$\sim$

Abbie was still fuming when she knocked off work and walked home that night. She was angry at Lachie for remembering, especially when she couldn't remember it herself. She was furious at him for confronting her at work, and she was terrified that he might try to take Hannah away from her.

She could leave Julia Creek. She could take Hannah back to Brisbane or even interstate. They would surely need nurses in rural New South Wales, or maybe some-where farther away like the Northern Territory or

Western Australia. Riley had said WA was beautiful. It would be a good place to hide.

But deep down, she knew she couldn't run from this. Secrets and lies always had a way of catching up with people, or so she'd heard.

She went through the motions that night with Hannah. She cooked her dinner and put her to bed, but all the while her mind was racing with what-ifs and maybes.

When Hannah was finally asleep in her room, Abbie pulled out her phone and dialled Paige's number.

"He remembers Birdsville."

"Huh? What?" Paige asked.

"We did sleep together, and Lachie remembers doing it."

"Are you sure he's telling the truth?"

"No, he's not lying. He remembers my birthmark. It's on my rib and not something I show or tell people about. He remembered its shape and exact location."

"Oh." Paige exhaled thoughtfully.

"He asked when Hannah's birthday is."

"What did you tell him?"

"Nothing. He confronted me at work, and I told him to leave me alone." Abbie slumped onto the couch and curled her legs under her.

"Maybe you should come clean. You said so yourself— he's a changed man, and maybe having Hannah in his life will keep him sober and responsible."

"Do you think so?" A spark of hope flickered to life.

"He's never been responsible for another person's happiness before. Sure, he's had the property but that's not the same. These country men take family values pretty seriously."

"I guess he deserves to know. What's the worst that could happen?"

"I think you need to lay it out. Give him the chance to walk away or be involved."

Abbie nodded, grateful she had asked her friend's advice.

"But you have to make this all about Hannah, which means you and him can't get involved. No matter what," Paige said.

"You're right," Abbie said resolutely. It was all about her daughter's happiness and what was best for Hannah.

She just hoped that Lachie would see it that way too.

CHAPTER 15

*A*bbie's heart thumped in her chest when she pulled up in front of Lachie's house the next day. She knew what she wanted to say and only hoped he would take the news well. Wings whooshed overhead as a group of cockatoos landed in the old eucalyptus tree.

Harriet waved from the kitchen window as Abbie approached the screen door.

"Hello. I wasn't expecting to see you today." The older woman said as she wiped her hands on her apron. The strong, homely smell of meat roasting warmed the air.

"I need to talk to Lachie. Is he around?" Abbie asked.

"He's repairing the chicken coup. A snake got in last night and ate one."

Abbie shivered. If there was one thing she hated it was snakes. Fortunately, living in town, she hadn't seen any yet.

"Just follow that path and you'll find him." Harriet pointed.

Abbie squared her shoulders and started toward the

coup. It didn't take long before she heard the *thud* of a hammer.

She paused for a moment and took in the sight of him nailing the chicken wire into a wooden post. He wore a navy singlet and his muscled arms gleamed with sweat. Dark patches stained his back. He was wearing a brown Akubra and dark sunglasses, so when he turned to her she couldn't see if he was shocked by her appearance on not.

"Hi Lachie."

He dropped the hammer and straightened, turning his body toward her. "I'm sorry about yesterday. I shouldn't have confronted you at work."

She shrugged. "I didn't give you much of a choice. I've been avoiding you."

"Yeah, I figured that much," he said. "Why?"

"Hannah was born on June the fourth." She let the words sink in.

"So Birdsville ..."

Abbie wrung her hands together. "I went to Birdsville to blow off some steam. I just wanted to be young and carefree for a change. I got plastered though and don't remember anything. A few weeks later, I found out I was pregnant and didn't have the first clue who the father was."

Lachie pulled off his sunglasses and tossed them on the ground before stepping toward her. "I remember us being together. I think I might be Hannah's father."

Anxiety had a way of stealing her words and her confidence when she least expected it. She forced herself to take two deep breaths before telling him the news that would upend his world. "As soon as you said you'd been to the same races, I started to wonder about that. Then I stole some hair from your brush so I could get a paternity test done."

"That's why you were in my room that day and acting so strange?" He raised his brows at her.

She nodded sheepishly. "I didn't want to worry you with my suspicions, especially if it turned out I was wrong."

He placed his finger under her chin so he could look straight in her eye. "What did the results say?"

She swallowed but her mouth was dry. "The results said that you are her father. Without a doubt."

When he remained silent, she continued talking. "I don't need anything. We're doing just fine."

He put a finger against her lips to silence her. "Without a doubt."

She had prepared herself for a variety of reactions, horror and disinterest being the main two. But he was anything but. His grin stretched from ear to ear as he bounced from leg to leg, punching the air, as if giddy with excitement.

Abbie couldn't help but giggle at him. "So, I take it you're alright with this?"

"Alright?" He turned to her, all seriousness now. "I never thought I wanted to be a dad as much as I have the last few days when I thought I might be. This is the best news I have ever had in my entire life." He put his hands on top of her shoulders. "Hannah is mine. Ours. We really are a family now."

"Yes, but listen to me, Lachie." She turned on her no-nonsense tone. "Hannah is everything to me. My whole life. If you want to be involved, you have to put her first too."

He nodded in reply.

"There have to be rules and boundaries. We have to make a plan."

"Okay. Yes, I understand." He moved closer as though to kiss her then, and she pulled back abruptly.

"That means that nothing can happen between us. We're parents not lovers."

His jaw tightened. "Why can't we be both? Why do you presume that us being together isn't the best thing for Hannah?"

She wanted to believe that. She wanted to have the happy, old-fashioned, traditional family. "I'm sure Hannah would love that, but if we broke up, she would be caught in the middle of it." She shook her head. "No. Parents only, nothing more." She extended her hand. "Deal?"

He studied her for a moment before slipping his hand in hers. "Fine. Now can we tell Mum? She'll be so excited."

∽

Lachie couldn't wipe the grin off his face as he and Abbie walked up the path to the house. This really was the best day of his life.

He was a dad.

Hannah Forsyth was his daughter.

He was the luckiest man in the world.

"What was she like as a baby?" He wanted to know everything. "How old was she when she started to walk? What was her first word?"

Abbie smiled back as only a proud mother could. "She was pretty good. I mean, she didn't sleep through the night until she was eight months old and I put her on formula."

His heart clenched. He had missed those late-night feedings, nappy changes, and watching his daughter grow from a baby into the little girl she was now. He had missed six years.

Six years he hadn't known she even existed.

"Her first word was Dadda," Abbie said tightly. "She said it to my father. I wasn't there for it."

Lachie stopped walking as his heart clenched. He should have been there. Hannah should have been calling him Dadda. "She called Adam Dadda?"

Abbie nodded. "I moved back in with them when I found out I was pregnant. My dad was the only man in her life for a long time."

Lachie liked and respected Adam Forsyth. He seemed a smart, sensible man and, unlike Lachie's own father, had a strong sense of family and commitment to putting their needs first.

Daniel McGuire had been an abusive drunk, and Lachie was glad he wouldn't be a part of his daughter's life.

Lachie held the door open for Abbie to enter the house in front of him, then they sat Harriet down for the news. She eyed them both with a furrowed brow. Harriet had always been a perceptive woman, she may have guessed already.

"It turns out Abbie and I met at the Birdsville Races

seven years ago," Lachie said, trying to avoid all the details he was sure his mother didn't really want to know.

"We'd both forgotten until recently," Abbie added.

Harriet nodded encouragingly.

Lachie threw caution to the wind and blurted out his news. "It turns out Hannah is actually my daughter."

Harriet's eyes widened in surprise. Nope, she hadn't seen this coming. "Your daughter Hannah?" She pointed at Abbie. "Is yours?" She turned to Lachie. "Which makes her my …"

"Your granddaughter." Abbie placed her hand on Harriet's and smiled kindly.

Harriet put her other hand to her heart. "That's incredible. I'm so happy."

The three exchanged hugs and congratulations. Lachie felt his heart bubble over with contentment.

Right now, life was good. He was happy, even if he couldn't be with Abbie right now. He had confidence that he would be able to win her over eventually.

Hannah was his priority and he was resolved to be the best father he could possibly be.

∼

Lachie followed Abbie back into town so they could tell Hannah together. He used the long drive to call his brothers and share the news. Noah was thrilled with the addition to the family and promised to make up for all the birthdays and Christmases they had missed.

Darcy put the phone on speaker, and Lachie told both

him and Meghan the news in a flurry of excitement and anticipation.

"Wow," Darcy exhaled. "Congratulations."

It was a disappointing reaction after Noah's excitement.

"I told you that you looked alike." Meghan's voice was flat, and it surprised him. She always tried to be so positive and upbeat.

"What's wrong? Has something happened?" Lachie asked.

He heard Meghan sob and then her voice got quieter as though she were running away from the phone.

"Are you there?" Lachie asked.

"Sorry, Lachie," Darcy said. "Meghan just had another miscarriage. She's not doing too well at the moment."

"Shit, I'm sorry." He felt like an asshole. This was probably the worst news she could get right now.

"It was early, and we'd tried not to get our hopes up. But it still hurts, you know?"

No, he didn't know. He'd spent his adult life trying not to impregnate the women he slept with. Now, without meaning to, he had a beautiful healthy daughter while his brother and sister-in-law were going through such a heart-wrenching experience.

"I guess we thought we'd be the first to give Mum a grandchild. It sounds silly-"

Lachie cut him off. "No, it doesn't. You guys are married and in love. Kids were always part of your plan and they still will be. I'm sure of it. What does the doctor say?"

Darcy sighed into the phone. "To keep trying. We're going for another round in a few weeks."

"Good luck. We're all here for you."

"Thanks and congratulations. Hannah is a great kid, and the offer is there if you want to bring her out here for a ride."

Lachie grinned, remembering Hannah's love of horses and all other farm animals. "She must get her horsemanship from our side of the family."

"From her uncles, you mean."

They said their goodbyes and Lachie ended the call. Just when his life was going so well, Darcy and Meghan were suffering the loss of another baby. Even if it was early in the pregnancy, he knew it must be a terrible thing to experience.

He wondered again at the gift he had been given. Abbie had a six-year head start on him. She knew all Hannah's likes and dislikes and different quirks. She had also had six years of worrying if her daughter was happy and healthy and wondering what kind of a woman she would grow into.

Lachie had missed six years. He didn't want to miss another moment.

～

"Maybe I should go buy her a toy first?" Lachie said when they pulled up in the driveway.

"She doesn't need any more toys, trust me," Abbie said, leading the way up to the house. It was almost three, and Hannah would be home soon. She would be so surprised to see Lachie here and even more surprised when she found out he was her father.

Harriet was so lovely and so were Lachie's brothers and their partners. It was a relief to know that Hannah shared their DNA and would have them in her life. She had sometimes feared the man she had slept with had been someone horrible and manipulative. But Lachie wasn't like that at all. He was kind to his neighbours and respectful of her wishes.

Inside the house, Lachie made coffee for them and a chocolate milk for Hannah while Abbie opened a packet of cream biscuits. "Special occasion," she said when she caught Lachie's eye.

When Hannah burst through the door, they were ready for her.

"Lachie!" She squealed and threw herself into his arms.

"Hey squirt."

"What are you doing here?"

"I missed you," he said and brushed her hair off her face. He studied her as if for the first time. She really did look like him. How had Abbie not realised it the moment she first saw him?

"Hannah, Lachie made you some chocolate milk." Abbie handed it to her and watched as she took a gulp.

"Thank you, Lachie."

"You're welcome." He kissed Hannah's forehead, and Abbie swallowed the lump in her throat.

He turned then and caught her eye. They hadn't had time to plan what to say. How did you explain something like this to a little kid?

She chose her words carefully. "Hannah, you know

how I always said your father lived a long way away and that was why you never met him?"

The little girl nodded and looked from one adult to the other.

"Well, sweetheart, Lachie is your father."

Hannah stopped slurping her milk and looked at him for confirmation. "You are?"

He grinned at her, shiny-eyed. "I am."

Hannah slowly stood and handed her cup to her mother before climbing back onto Lachie's lap and wrapping her arms around his neck. "My Christmas wish came early."

"What?" she asked.

Hannah looked at Abbie. "I already started wishing that Santa would make Lachie my new father."

Lachie chuckled and Abbie felt her cheeks warm.

"Does that mean you two will get married?" she asked Lachie very seriously.

"No, not right now at least." He looked at Abbie like he wanted nothing more. It caused Abbie's heart to race once more with the idea that this was where she truly belonged. Not in the city with the constant hum of activity and people. But at Brigadier Station. In the small outback town where Hannah's father and their family lived.

Hannah shrugged. "Can I at least call you Dad?"

Lachie nodded enthusiastically. "Yes please."

"I love you, Dad."

"I love you too, squirt."

CHAPTER 16

*A*bbie yawned her way through story time that night with Hannah. It had been a big day for all of them, but Hannah was coping with the news well.

"Will we move to Lachie's house?" she asked as Abbie snuggled in for a cuddle.

"What? No."

"Why not? I'd like to live there."

Abbie's guts churned. "Because we live here. I go to work here and you go to school here. Things won't change that much."

"But I could do School of the Air like Brooke and Scotty," she said, referring to two of Paige's step-children.

"But I still have to go to work. That would be a long drive for me."

Hannah nodded and fell silent for just a moment. "Can I at least have sleepovers out there?"

"We'll see." Abbie stroked her daughter's hair. She knew she would have to compromise on things like sleepovers and holidays, but she didn't want to worry about that right now.

Hannah finally had a father, and of course they would want to spend time together. Lachie would be able to teach Hannah things and share experiences with her that Abbie wouldn't be a part of.

Abbie wouldn't be the centre of her daughter's life anymore. She would have to get used to sharing that role with Lachlan McGuire.

The control freak in Abbie reared its ugly head. After all, that was the whole reason they had left Brisbane. Her parents had become too involved and too opinionated about how she chose to raise her daughter. It was one thing coming from her parents, but coming from Lachie … she wasn't sure how she would handle it.

A lot had changed since Abbie and Hannah had moved to Julia Creek. Gone were the days of high society and housekeepers. Abbie's parents had promised they wouldn't interfere with Abbie's style of parenting, that they would complement it. Abbie should have known better. As soon as she'd moved back into their riverside townhouse in Brisbane, single and with a baby on the way, they had started making arrangements. It had taken five years for the tensions to finally boil over. So when the opportunity came for Abbie to continue her nursing career in outback Queensland, she had jumped at the chance. Her daughter, always one for adventure, had happily agreed, even though it meant leaving the only home she had ever known and her beloved grandparents.

But it had turned out alright. Hannah was happy here. She was having a true country childhood where she could run around barefoot, swim in creeks, and go to public school with kids of various upbringings and financial situations. Not that preppy private school her grandmother had enrolled her in.

"I can't wait for Father's Day," Hannah said, her voice deep with sleep. "This will be the first time we can celebrate it."

"Yes it will be," Abbie whispered into her hair. "And his first too."

∼

It had been a long time since Lachie had walked the grounds of the Julia Creek State School. It looked like not too much had changed. It was still a small country school doing the best that it could for its community.

He didn't recognise any of the other parents waiting to collect their children. They were grouped together, chatting and gossiping, and he couldn't help but feel like a fish out of water.

He didn't care what people thought though. He was here for Hannah and Hannah alone.

He perused the posters on the door. One caught his eye, inviting parents to a reading competition. He made a mental note of the time and date.

"Lachie? What are you doing here?"

He turned to see the local butcher and grinned.

"G'day, Johnno."

Johnno greeted him with a frown. "Since when do you have kids?"

Lachie smiled, unable to keep the pride from his voice. "I just found out myself. My daughter is Hannah Forsyth."

"Really? Hannah Forsyth? She and my daughter Lilly are good mates." Johnno narrowed his gaze. "So you and Abbie then?"

Lachie nodded. The word was going to get out sooner or later, so he might as well explain the full story. "We used to know each other. But it wasn't until recently that we made the connection."

Johnno put his hands on his hips and raised his eyebrows like he knew there was more to the story. "Well, congratulations. Hannah's a great kid. She comes over for play dates all the time, mate."

"Thanks. We should get your family out to Brigadier Station then."

"That'd be great. Always wondered what the big deal was about." Johnno winked as the school bell chimed and the doors were swung open.

Little people came flying out, huge bags on their backs and excited expressions on their faces. Lachie searched the uniformed children until he spotted Hannah's long blonde locks.

"Daddy," she said and ran up to hug him. Adults everywhere turned to watch with wide eyes.

Yep, the news was definitely out.

"Hey squirt. How was school?"

"Good. I didn't know you were picking me up."

"I asked your mum if it'd be okay if we spent the afternoon together and she said yes."

Abbie had had to think about it and make him promise to stay in town.

"Do you want to meet my teacher, Mrs. Phillips? She's really nice."

"Sure," he said and followed her inside the classroom.

When they were finished meeting Hannah's teacher, and Lachie had learned how good a student Hannah was and how well liked she was, they finally strolled out the gates, hand in hand.

"I'm hungry," Lachie said, "How about we go to the bakery for a snack?"

"Can I have a lamington?" Hannah beamed.

"Lamingtons sound perfect." He swung her arm and she giggled, the sound touching his heart in a way he'd never expected.

How was it possible to love another person so completely and feel so protective of them? He might not have been a father long but he planned to make up for it by being the best one possible.

~

Lachie treasured every precious moment he spent with Hannah over the next few weeks. Abbie allowed their daughter to stay at Brigadier Station overnight on the weekends while she was working, and Lachie took the opportunity to teach Hannah all about farm life. So far they had watched chicks hatch out of eggs and found a stray cat and her kittens take up residence in their shed.

"It's not just about looking after the animals. We've got to look after the land too," he explained as they tended Harriet's veggie patch together. Hannah had wanted to try growing lettuces, so together they had bought the seedlings and tended them.

"Will they be ready soon?"

Lachie studied the small green leaves. "In another couple of weeks I'd say."

"Then we can make Mum a green salad. Gran said we can use her tomatoes and cucumber too," Hannah said.

Lachie smiled. "I bet your Mum will love it. I know how much she likes her salads."

"Dad, can we go camping?"

He handed her the watering can. "Sure, squirt. Have you ever been camping before?"

"No, but I think I'd like to sleep under the stars."

He stood back and surveyed his daughter in her new work jeans and the bright pink work shirt Harriet had ordered online. Lachie had even bought her a child's size Akubra. She really looked the part of an outback kid now.

"We'll ask your mum. Maybe she'll want to come too."

Hannah just laughed. Lachie didn't think Abbie would like the idea much either. She had probably never camped a night in her life. But that didn't diminish his opinion of her in any way.

He had been finding her more attractive than ever. Lachie often found himself staring at her and wishing they didn't have this stupid rule about not dating. It was killing him not to touch her and kiss her whenever he saw her. She showed so much love and affection to her daughter, and he craved it for himself as well.

Hannah handed Lachie back the empty watering can. "Now what?"

He grinned at her. "Have you ever been on a quad bike?"

～

Abbie was in a good mood as her car rattled over the cattle grid and pulled up outside Lachie's house. The last few weeks had been amazing and filled with happy memories they would all cherish.

As well as Hannah and Lachie spending plenty of good-quality one-on-one time together, they had also done things together, just the three of them. She couldn't deny her heart was softening to Lachie. How could it not when he was being so kind and respectful of her decision not to get involved romantically.

Only, the more she tried to fight her feelings, the stronger they grew. Her resolve was crumbling. Maybe she was being too cautious after all.

Maybe they could have the happiness Lachie was so confident in. After all, he had compromised about so many things. Maybe she could let herself take a chance on love.

Abbie glanced at her watch. They had agreed that Lachie would bring Hannah home tonight, but she had finished work early and was lonely by herself so had decided to surprise them.

"Abbie, great to see you." Harriet stood from pruning the rose bushes and came over to hug her. "I thought Lachie was dropping Hannah off today?"

Abbie opened her mouth to explain when she heard the roar of an engine. She and Harriett both turned and watched as Lachie drove up the dirt path on his quad bike, Hannah perched in front of him.

Fury burned in the back of her throat. "What is he doing?"

Harriet shrugged. "They've been having a great time."

"But she's not even wearing a helmet." Abbie stormed off towards them and Lachie slowed to a stop.

"Hey, Mum's here." Lachie said.

"What the hell is she doing on this thing?" She didn't try to quell the anger she felt. "Hannah, get off now."

Lachie held up his hands. "What's the problem? She's fine."

"Don't tell me she's fine. These things are dangerous. Do you know how many injuries I see because people are riding these death traps?" Abbie stalked forward and pulled her daughter into her arms. She felt herself shaking with anger and something else. Disappointment?

Lachie killed the engine and swung off the quad. "Don't stress. I've been riding all my life. This is what kids do in the bush."

"Not my kid," she spat at him and turned on her heel.

"Mum, you're squeezing me." Hannah twisted.

Abbie kissed her forehead and put her down. "You go inside with Gran and get your things. We're going home."

"But we were going to make dinner." Hannah pouted.

"Now." Abbie thrust out her arm and pointed towards the house.

Her daughter walked away, shoulders rounded.

When she was out of hearing range, Abbie twirled back to Lachie. He had come up behind her though, and she slammed into him. He caught her in his arms and for a moment she forgot her anger and just wanted to savour the sensation.

"I'm sorry," he said gently and turned her chin up to face him.

Abbie swallowed hard, then remembered what he'd done. She pushed him away with a strength even she didn't know she had. "You put her life in danger."

"I didn't. I swear she was safe the whole time. We didn't go very fast."

"She never should have been on it. You should have asked me."

She watched as Lachie inhaled slowly. "She's my daughter too. I get some say in this."

The floodgates opened, and she couldn't control the anger she unleashed. "She was my daughter first. I raised her so it's my decision. You've been her father for five bloody minutes so don't tell me I don't know what's best for her."

Turning her back on him, Abbie practically ran to the house.

But he was right behind her, grabbing her arm. She tried to pull away, but he was too strong.

"That wasn't my fault, was it? If I'd known about her then I could have been there." His anger met hers now, the pain of the past and missed years surfacing.

She tried to refocus the argument. "It's illegal to take a child on a quad bike."

"And I said I'm sorry. I won't do it again." He knocked his Akubra off his head and clasped his head in frustration.

"Damn right you won't," she said snakily before going

in for the kill. "Maybe you're not fit to be a father after all."

The moment the words were out, she regretted them. She covered her mouth with her hand and watched as Lachie paled.

"So that's how you really feel? That she's better off without me?" His voice was defeated and his whole posture slumped like she had just punched him hard in the gut.

"No, I—"

"Don't." He waved his hand at her. "Take her then." He scooped up his hat before climbing back onto his bike and revving the engine.

She moved towards him, apologies on her tongue. But he cast her a defeated look before spinning the quad and speeding away.

Shit. She had gone too far. She had let her anger get the better of her and had hurt someone she cared about.

And she did care about Lachie McGuire.

More than she'd realised until this exact moment.

CHAPTER 17

*T*hat was a low blow Lachie hadn't seen coming from Abbie. Even if she'd been thinking it, he never would have expected her to say it to his face like that.

"Maybe you're not fit to be a father after all."

He couldn't get her voice out of his head. Those words had wounded him more deeply than anything else ever had.

Not even the rejection of being left at the alter by Meghan had been as bad as this. He was reminded of how unpredictable life could be and how it could change in a heartbeat.

He wanted to smash something, to yell and scream. But most of all, he wanted a drink.

Not just one drink. He wanted to drink until he felt numb again. Until he forgot the horror of his father's abuse; Dylan's death; and Abbie's gut-wrenching words.

He spun the quad sharply, throwing up dust before driving into the shed and killing its engine.

He paused next to his ute. He could drive into town. The pub was open, and he was sure he'd be welcomed back.

He could already taste the bitter alcohol at the back of his throat.

There was nothing and no one to stop him now.

∼

The knocking on her front door pulled Abbie from her restless regrets. She had picked up the phone and started to call Lachie several times to apologise to him, to tell him just how much she regretted saying those things. That they weren't true.

She glanced down the hallway to Hannah's room. The door was still closed and she should be sound asleep. The argument with Lachie, then the one they'd had on the way home, had left her worn out.

She opened the front door and surveyed the tall figure in the doorway. Stubble shadowed Lachie's chin and his dark hair was tousled like he'd tunnelled a hand through the front. It had only been a few hours since their last encounter but he looked like he'd aged in that time.

"Lachie?" She exhaled deeply as she took him in. That look of complete despair seemed to weigh his shoulders down. He appeared defeated.

"Can I come in?"

She nodded and stepped aside. He walked past her and sat on the couch. She followed, sitting in the space next to him.

She covered his hand with her own. "I'm so sorry for what I said."

He looked down at their hands for a moment before raising those cerulean-blue eyes to hers.

Abbie swallowed hard. His guards were down and she could see right into his soul. She had never seen him so vulnerable. It made her feel even more ashamed.

"What you said about being a bad father …" His voice was raw. "Cutting off my arm would have hurt less."

Tears stung her eyes and Abbie blinked them back.

"My dad was a horrible man. I didn't know how horrible until last year when Mum finally told us how she'd been abused and how Noah and Darcy had been beaten up and mistreated. Daniel had always been different with me, so I hadn't seen it. Now I do." He turned her hand over in his and held it with both of his. "I don't want to be like my dad. If you really think Hannah is better off without me then I'll walk away now and never see her again. If that's what you want, I'll do it."

"No." She sobbed out the word, then flung her arms around him. "You're a great father. She's so lucky to have you." Her words were muffled as she spoke against the softness of his neck.

His arms tightened around her back. "Are you sure?"

She nodded. She breathed in the musky smell of him, then moved her hand up his back and into his hair. It felt so good to be this close to him. She'd missed it so much.

"Abbie." Her name came out on a sigh.

In reply, she pushed closer to him and pressed soft kisses against his neck, his pulse quickening under her lips.

He pulled her more fully onto him and leaned back, surrendering to her. She relished the power. Straddling his hips, she stared into his eyes. Lust had replaced agony.

Abbie had no idea who moved first. All she knew was that she was in his arms and this time, kissing him wasn't going to be enough. When his mouth left hers and he grabbed her hand to tug her along the hallway towards her room, she knew that he felt exactly the same way.

With the bedroom door safely locked behind them, Lachie slid his hands up under her shirt until they spanned her ribcage, his thumbs resting against the underside of her breasts. She leaned into him, thankful she had already changed out of her bra. He skimmed his hands higher, palming her softness, uttering a moan she echoed. She let him pull her T-shirt up and over her head, revealing her naked body above her shorts.

When she lifted her hands to his shirt, he tugged it over his head and tossed it aside. She splayed her hands over his chest. It felt so good to be touching him, feeling his muscles ripple under her fingers. Being able to explore every inch. She had no fears or concerns about what was about to happen. She'd never been so sure of anything in her life. She wriggled out of her shorts before turning to help him.

When they were naked, Lachie led her to the bed and knelt between her thighs. He leaned down and kissed her. Abbie moaned at the electricity between them, every-where they touched. He trailed kisses over her mouth, her jaw, down the side of her neck, and into the hollow at the base of her throat. She thrust her hands through his hair as he continued his journey south. His fingers touched her sensitive, wet nerves moments before his tongue.

Her hand flew to her mouth, muffling sounds she couldn't contain. His expert strokes and licks brought her to the edge within minutes.

As she recovered, her body still tingling, he looked up at her. Her face was warm but need still surged through her. She reached for him and he responded by nuzzling her neck and kissing her again.

"Condom?" he asked when he came up for air.

"Nightstand." She waited as he rustled around in the drawer before tearing open a packet and moving to push the condom on himself.

Ready, she cradled him between her thighs and he moved slowly, pushing inside her. She savoured every sensation as pleasure spread through her again. She met each thrust with a lift of her hips, bringing him deeper into her. He moaned as his lips found her breast. She urged him on, moved against him, opened up to him until he lost control. They went over the edge together, both of them crying out, neither bothering to hold back until Lachie finally collapsed beside her, breathing hard. She rolled and cuddled up against him, not wanting to break physical contact. He tucked her under his arm. She smiled as she listened to his heartbeat finally slow to a normal rhythm.

In this moment, everything was perfect. Everything else would work itself out.

~

Lachie held her close to him, content and happy with her safe in his arms. Right from the start she'd affected him like no other woman ever had. She made him feel deep emotions of happiness, joy, contentment. He could spend a lifetime loving her and he knew it still would never be enough.

She wiggled her bottom against his hips, and he felt his body stir. He drew in a deep, slow breath, hoping to quell the unexpected fluttering low in his belly.

"I'm glad you came over last night," she said into the stillness of the early morning.

"Me too." He kissed her bare shoulder. "Abbie, I need to tell you something."

He felt her tense before she rolled over to look at him with wide eyes. "What?"

Lachie swallowed. He needed to tell her everything. There could be no lies or half-truths between them. "I didn't plan on coming here when I left the station. I was going to the pub. I wanted to get so drunk that I'd forget everything."

In the dim light of the lamp, he watched as guilt clouded her face. "I'm sorry."

He reached out and stroked her cheek. "No, I am. I've been bottling things up—what my father did to us; Dylan's death. Then the thought of losing you and Hannah …" He choked back the emotion building in his throat.

"But you came here instead?"

He nodded. "Instead of going to the pub, I found myself on your doorstep."

She kissed his cheek. "Thank you for your honesty. I

know what addiction is like. I've had lots of patients with lots of different addictions. I know how hard it is to live with. The battle you face every day. I'm sorry if I made it more difficult for you."

He picked up her hand and tenderly kissed her fingertips, one at a time. "It's because of you and Hannah that I will stay sober every day for the rest of my life. This I promise you." He vowed. "You make me want to be a better man. And even though you deserve someone better, without all this baggage and these complications, I want to make myself worthy of you and Hannah. Because I love you, and I love the family we have together." The words flowed from him. He was more vulnerable and unguarded than he had ever been before. But every word he spoke was honest and raw.

Abbie's jaw trembled and her voice was husky. "I promise I will help you to fight those demons and I'll remind you every day of all the good things you have in your life and how much you are cherished and loved. Because you are, Lachie. You really, really are."

He pulled her close as relief rolled through him. He found her lips and with his kisses, he promised her his heart, body, and soul. He knew that there were never any guarantees in life. Sometimes you just had to take a risk.

He was willing to risk everything for his family, and judging by the way she kissed him back, so was Abbie.

～

Kookaburras sang their merry song from the tree outside Abbie's bedroom, and the brilliant sunshine poured through the gap in her curtains like a golden river. She snuggled closer into Lachie's warm embrace. He was still there. He hadn't scurried off in the middle of the night like other men had. No, Lachie wasn't here for a night of lust between the sheets. He had said he was here for the long term and she believed him.

She closed her eyes and tried to picture their future together. How many mornings would she wake up just like this, by his side, anticipating the day? On occasions Hannah might join them for early morning snuggles with both her parents, and they would chat about school and their new life together.

Perhaps, one day, Hannah might have a younger sibling to boss around.

Lachie moved and placed a warm kiss on her forehead. She moaned and lifted her face, seeking his mouth on her own. Wanting more of the pleasure he had so generously given her already.

Breathing heavily, Lachie dragged his mouth from her lips, then cruised the line of her jaw and down her neck. Her breasts swelled, heavy and aching, desperate for his touch.

Sounds of Hannah moving around outside their door had them both pausing. A look at Lachie made them both smother giggles, like they were sneaky teenagers, about to be caught.

"Do you want me to leave?" Lachie asked.

Abbie kissed him gently before shaking her head. "No."

He made to roll out of bed but she placed her hand on his arm. "Lachie, promise me something?"

"Anything." He stroked her cheek.

"If things don't work out between us, no matter what, we have to put Hannah's needs and wellbeing first."

His eyes were serious as he looked back at her. "Of course. I'll never do anything to hurt her."

She let out a breath before pulling him in for another kiss. "I know you wouldn't."

They climbed out of bed and dressed, Lachie in yesterday's clothes and Abbie in her uniform. How she would get through today with Lachie on her mind, she didn't know.

Abbie left the room first and busied herself in the kitchen, preparing breakfast and hot drinks.

"Good morning," she said as she kissed the top of her daughter's head when she entered.

"Morning," her daughter replied sleepily before sitting at the table and digging in to her bowl of soggy Weet-Bix.

Then Lachie walked into the kitchen and it was as though it was the most natural thing in the world for him to be there with them.

Hannah looked up and rubbed her eyes. "Dad?"

He went to her and hugged her. "Morning squirt. How'd you sleep?"

She looked between her parents, her little brain no doubt trying to understand what had happened. "You slept over?"

"Is that okay?" Lachie asked as he grabbed an apple from the fruit bowl and munched into it.

A crease appeared between her eyes, identical to her father's. "But yesterday you had a big argument."

Abbie crouched in front of her daughter and put her hand on her arm. "Daddy came over last night and we talked it over. We both apologised for the mean things we said."

Hannah looked to Lachie for affirmation.

He nodded. "It's all forgiven now. Are we good?" He directed the question at Hannah, who grinned in reply.

Abbie hugged her daughter. "Daddy might stay over more often, if that's okay with you." She hoped her daughter agreed, because she didn't want to miss out on nights like last night in the future.

Hannah bounced in her seat. "He could move in. I'd be fine with that."

"Good to know." Lachie winked at Abbie who grinned back.

Abbie rose to stand beside Lachie. He reached for her hand. They were in this together. A team. "For now, we're just going to date and hang out together. We'll see where it leads."

Hannah smiled as though all her birthdays and Christmases had come at once. "Sounds like a great idea to me."

CHAPTER 18

*L*achie spent the day steadily working through his list of jobs. The sooner he was done, the sooner he could head back into town. Right now, he was tensioning a barbed wire fence in the paddock near the windmill, the sun warm on his shoulders.

He had awoken with a new outlook on life. This was his second chance and by God, he wasn't going to waste a second of it. He had nearly lost Abbie and Hannah last night and he knew, without a doubt, that he needed them in his life. They were his life raft. His reason for everything.

He inhaled deeply, filling his lungs with the earthy smells of the bush: dust, eucalypt, cattle, and fresh country air. This was the life for him. A life of hard, physical, and yet rewarding labour. A life surrounded by his children and his family. A life where his roots were embedded in the history of Brigadier Station.

Eventually this drought would pass and he would bring back his cattle and continue his breeding program.

He had learned from his past mistakes and was adamant not to repeat them again. The booze was behind him. He had also decided to schedule in regular appointments with the counsellor. He had to keep on top of his own health, both physical and mental, if he was going to be able to look after his family and their future.

Together they would work through the obstacle of distance and find time to be together. There was still so much he wanted to learn about Abbie and Hannah and he couldn't wait to start discovering.

His phone buzzed in his pocket and he wiped his hands before fishing it out of his jeans and answering the call. "Brigadier Station."

"Hi Lachie, it's Maddie."

His heart tightened as it always did when he spoke to his friend's widow. Just hearing her voice reminded him of that day. The day he had tried to forget but which still woke him sometimes at night.

"Hi. How are you?"

She paused as though searching for words. How was she? How would she ever be okay after what had happened? "I just wanted to let you know that we're moving back to Mt Isa. We'll live with Mum while I find a job."

Lachie had known it was coming. The station had been up for sale for a few weeks now. Maddie couldn't look after the station plus the kids and on no income. Dylan had left her in a rotten situation. She had barely been able to pay for the funeral and other expenses.

"We'll be sorry to lose you. How can I help?"

"Is there anything here you can use? Equipment or

feed?" Her voice was desperate, and he knew she *was* desperate. "The bank will probably end up selling the place for half of what it's worth, so you may as well take whatever you can."

He agreed to come over and even though she didn't want any payment, he would give her a fair price. When he was finished on the phone, he sat and watched the landscape around him. An emu emerged from some scrub and scampered on its long legs and wide-splayed toes across the brown dirt in front of him.

Life on the land was hard and not everyone was cut out for it. Abbie was a city girl. She managed just fine in town where she was surrounded by people, but how would she go out here? Did she have the resilience and patience to wait out a drought? When the floods came, would she be prepared to be isolated for weeks without power?

Being with Lachie meant being on the land and loving it for all it offered and all it took away. Was she really up for the challenge? Did she even understand the hardships?

As much as she'd promised him she'd be there for him, what if this life was too much? Too hard? What if it broke her, like it had broken Dylan?

∼

Lachie loaded the last of the machinery parts onto the back of his ute. He had found lots of spare parts and bits and pieces of Dylan's that may come in handy one day. He was just tying down the tarp as the sound of an engine approached.

He watched as Abbie climbed out of her car. The way her face lit up when she spotted him warmed him all the way to his soul. Hannah emerged from the back seat and reached her father first, hugging him hello. He squeezed her back, listening as she quickly told him all about her day, then asked if she could go and play with Emma and Jamie.

"Sure you can. They're inside with Maddie." He waved at his neighbour's house. This would be the last time visiting them.

The shipping container stood next to the homestead, packed to the top with the family's belongings and memories.

"It's hard to believe that a lifetime can be packed up in just a few days," Abbie said, her gaze following his to the container.

"Yep. Even at the worst of times, I never thought it would come to this. The money from the rodeo helped, but without any stock …" His voice trailed off. His father had always had back-up plans. He had shares in the stock market and other long-term investments. Drought-proofing had been taught to Lachie from a young age and as much as he despised his father, he was thankful for the keen business sense he'd been taught. But just because he was a little bit like his father didn't mean he had to be exactly like him.

Abbie curled her arms around him. "I know it's hard. I'm going to miss them too."

He stroked her hair. "You see what Maddie's going through? Lots of people are going through the same thing. Country life is hard. Long days which drain a man physically and emotionally." He raised her chin so she was looking at him. "Are you cut out for this? Is it a life you want?"

She bit her lip and loosened her arms. "I don't know." She stepped away and gestured to the landscape around her. "I wasn't expecting to like it so much here, to be so accepted by the community." She looked back at him. "And I definitely wasn't expecting to fall in love."

His heart skipped a beat at her declaration of love. "I don't want you to be unhappy out here. That would be worse for me than not having you in my life."

She raised her hand and lifted the tip of his Akubra up. "Some things are worth all the hard work. I believe you are one of those things, and I want to try to make a life with you out here."

He raised her hand to his lips. "That's the best we can hope for."

They turned and walked to the tired old house. There was precious little left inside, and they chatted about Maddie's plans over tea and biscuits brought over from Brigadier Station.

"The kids can go to school for a change. Emma's been doing School of the Air her whole life so she's a bit nervous." Maddie looked at her teenage step-daughter. The poor girl had been abandoned by her birth mother as a baby, and now her father was gone too. She wouldn't have an easy life going forward, even with her step-mother's love.

Little Jamie was still a toddler, not even three yet. He wouldn't even remember the place or his life out here.

Hannah walked Jamie over to the adults, holding his

hand in hers. The little boy looked just like his father with his jet-black hair and dark brown eyes.

"Bickey?" Jamie asked.

Maddie handed her son one of Harriet's famous Anzac biscuits, and they all watched as he bit into the crunchy treat.

"Babies always have a way of being the centre of attention, don't they?" Lachie said as he watched the child. He wondered what Hannah had been like at that age.

"Mummy and Daddy are dating," Hannah said to Maddie like it was news everyone ought to know. "I hope they have a baby one day. I'd like to be a big sister."

Abbie clapped her hand over her mouth and Lachie chuckled. He would like nothing more than to fill Brigadier Station with their children, especially if they were as forward and charming as their firstborn.

Maddie smiled but it was as though she had forgotten how to. "You might get your wish one day. I hope you'll be a good girl for your parents."

"I will." Hannah hugged Maddie and kissed her on the cheek. "Will you come back and visit us?"

Maddie forced a smile. "Maybe one day, but until then you can come and visit us in Mt Isa whenever you want."

Hannah led Jamie back to the couch where a small pile of toys waited for them.

Lachie leaned forward on his knees and stared into his empty cup. "It won't be the same without you."

Maddie sighed. "I thought I'd be like Harriet and live out my days in this house. We'd watch our children have children and teach them about living in the bush." Lachie watched as she wiped away a tear. "But I can't do it without Dylan."

Abbie moved to her friend's side and hugged her.

Change was the only constant out here, and you had to be able to adapt. Over time, Maddie and the children would get used to their new life in town.

And, hopefully, Abbie would adapt to living in the outback with him. Only time would tell if they could last the distance or whether this life he loved so much was too much for the city girl he had fallen head over heels for.

CHAPTER 19

*A*bbie and Lachie slipped into an easy routine. He spent most nights at her house in town so as not to disrupt Hannah's school routine. But, with holidays fast approaching, they were planning for some full-time station life with Abbie taking time off too.

Since their conversation at Maddie's, Abbie had been seriously considering the obstacles and realities of remote country life. Long phone conversations with both Paige and Meghan had given her a dose of much-needed reality. Although still apprehensive, Abbie knew she had a better understanding of what a future with Lachie would entail. She would have to compromise on certain things she took for granted, but she also knew the payoff would be worth it.

Lachie came to sit with her on the couch after putting their daughter to bed. He stretched out and gathered her to him. "What have you got there?"

She presented him with the large book she had been holding, waiting to share with him. "I don't know why I haven't shown you this earlier." She opened it to the first page: a photo of Abbie in a blue bikini, proudly showing off her pregnant belly.

Lachie straightened next to her and leaned in to better study the photograph. "You were huge."

She laughed at his comment. "I went into labour the very next day."

He looked at her. "Did you like being pregnant?"

"I loved it. She moved around all the time, reminding me I was never alone."

His lips curled up, then he returned to the album and turned the page. Photos of the pink, wrinkly newborn and her mother covered the next few sheets, and Lachie took his time studying each one.

Abbie lay her head on Lachie's shoulder. "What do you think?"

He looked up and she was shocked to see his eyes glazed over. "I think we made the most beautiful baby in the world."

She pressed her lips against his. "Me too."

"Would you have more?"

"Babies?" She bit her lip as he nodded. "Yeah, I'd like another one or two."

Relief relaxed his jaw.

They continued looking through the pictures and Abbie told him stories, sharing the most intimate details of her life so that he might understand her better and feel like even though he wasn't there, he knew exactly what happened.

He turned to the last page and his breath caught as he

saw the latest picture. It was their very first family photo, taken at the rodeo with Zoe Gilmore.

His finger traced around the edges. "Look at us." He exhaled.

"That's when we went from a family of two to a family of three."

He turned to her. "Thank you for showing me these. I feel more a part of your lives now."

"You're welcome." She tenderly stroked the soft hairs of his five o'clock shadow. She couldn't wait to ditch every item of clothing. She wanted to run her hands over his hard muscles and gaze upon him naked. She deftly sneaked her hands under his shirt, loving the heat blasting from his skin. His desire for her was immediately clear as he pulled her onto his lap, and her hunger for him flared hot.

"Let's take this to the bedroom." The yearning in his voice kicked her pulse up higher. She climbed off him and led him down the hall. Inside her room, he grabbed her waist and spun her around so she slammed into his chest, winded. She looked up at him through her lashes before his mouth crashed onto hers. Abbie melted against him. A fire of need kindled hot inside her.

When Lachie reached between them to undo the buttons of her shirt, she found the hem of his and urged it up over his head. Soon both shirts were discarded on the floor. He ran a finger along the lace edge of her bra, and Abbie's breath caught. When he reached around to unclasp it, she gladly let him take it off. It joined the growing pile of their clothes, and Abbie moaned as Lachie massaged her breasts. Her nipples were already hard, and each stroke of his hand over her sensitive skin brought another wave of desire through her. When he bent to take one nipple into his mouth, Abbie closed her eyes and arched her back. His touch sent waves of heat flooding through her system and she yearned for more, to have his hands everywhere on her body. He took his time exploring her, teasing her nipples and loving them with his tongue.

Abbie wrestled with the belt and button of Lachie's jeans. He was so hard when she got him free, she was in no doubt of how he felt about her.

"I want to be inside you." His ragged voice undid her.

"I want that, too, but first." She raised a mischievous eyebrow at him before pushing him onto the bed and hovering over his hips. She captured him in her mouth and swirled her tongue around his tip. With a groan, his fingers threaded through her hair, urging her deeper, and she obliged with a hungry need. She teased him toward the edge, her hands rubbing and stroking his base until he started to squirm. Sitting up, she reached for a condom and rolled it onto his throbbing hardness.

He lifted her on top of him and shifted into place before pushing inside, filling her in the most exquisite way. When he began to move, it took everything she had not to come right then. He was so hard and thick. With her hands on his chest, her hips moving up and down, she met his gaze and tried to show him everything she was feeling; how happy he made her and how much pleasure he gave her.

His muscles rippled as he gripped her hips, guiding her movements, speeding her up. Abbie cried out as the delicious friction sent her over the edge. Lachie bucked with his release before pulling her down on top of him.

She pushed away the whisper of doubt in the back of her head, and focused on the sound of his breathing. The rise and fall of his chest under her cheek. Lachie had a tenderness, a kindness he didn't usually let show.

He might be a proud, outback man, but he was her man, and she liked him just the way he was.

CHAPTER 20

*A*bbie sat on the veranda overlooking the brown paddocks of Brigadier Station, filling her lungs with clean, fresh, morning air. These last few days staying on the property with Lachie and Harriet had been some of the happiest of her life.

She smiled as Lachie stepped through the door and walked towards her. He was dressed in low-slung faded jeans, his open shirt revealing a fine line of inky hair which ran from his waistband and curled around his neat belly button before trailing toward his chest. The pale bronze skin of his torso stretched smooth over taut, well-developed muscles.

"Morning." He stood with his arms wrapped around her from behind, hugging her protectively as he kissed the top of her head.

She leaned into him and sighed. "What's on today's agenda?"

"Hannah wants to help me finish the treehouse." His breath was warm on her ear. Lachie had asked Abbie's permission before telling Hannah his plans to build her the treehouse. He'd been so excited about making her something with his own two hands. "It'll be her private place," he'd said. "My brothers and I built one when Noah was about her age, and we played in it all the time. Until Dad pulled it down when we were away at boarding school." The light in his eyes had faded while talking about his father.

Abbie had agreed so long as it wasn't built too high off the ground, and there were no nasty nails sticking out or other construction hazards that could cause injury. Lachie and Hannah had spent all day yesterday working on it together, and when Abbie had asked to see it they had refused, telling her it would be a surprise.

"She asked me if she could live in it," he said. "It made me think that we should give her a room of her own."

"She has a room here," Abbie said. Hannah was currently still asleep in the spare room next to theirs. The room her Uncle Darcy had used until moving to Arabella Plains.

"Yeah, but it's not very girly. I was thinking we could paint it and buy some new furniture. Get her to choose some pretty sheets, that kind of thing."

Just when she thought she couldn't love him anymore, Lachie said something like that. "I think Hannah would love a pony themed bedroom."

She turned in his arms, wanting to see him. It was the warmth that filled his face when he looked at their daughter, the joy that sparkled in his eyes when he laughed, and the affection he showered on them without any care of what anyone thought of them that made her so happy things had worked out this way. "If Hannah gets her own room, maybe I could add a few things to your room?"

He brushed a kiss over her nose. "What did you have in mind?"

"Hm, maybe some new sheets and a pretty mat for the floor."

He nodded. "You can do whatever you want. I even think we should move some of my clothes out of the wardrobe so you can put yours in there."

She looped her arms around his neck. "You want to give me space in your wardrobe? You must really like me."

"Nah, I don't like you." He narrowed his gaze. "I love you, Abbie."

She looked into his eyes and saw in them the love he'd declared so plainly.

"I love you too." Nothing had ever been so right. Of course they were meant to be together. Would she ever stop feeling this much love for him? She doubted it, as he bent to kiss her. And then all she could think about was Lachie.

~

Lachie checked the sheets fully covered the treehouse one more time as he heard Harriet and Abbie approach. With her wind-tousled hair and dressed in faded farm clothes, he'd never seen Abbie looking more beautiful.

Hannah held his hand as she bounced beside him. Her Akubra was perched at an angle on her head. "Do you think she'll like it?"

He kneeled down next to her and straightened the hat. "I reckon she'll love it almost as much as you do."

Hannah giggled and Lachie straightened to greet the women. "Welcome to the unveiling."

Harriet looked on eagerly. "Come on then. I'm not getting any younger."

Abbie nodded at him and he reached over and tugged on the sheets, revealing the pale wooden treehouse with the varnished wooden stairs and arched window frames.

"Wow." Abbie studied the building for a moment before Hannah took her hand and led her inside. It only stood a metre off the dirt and encircled the old gum tree near the chicken coup.

"I can bring the chickens in here when I want to play with them," Hannah said, brushing her hand across the windowsill.

"As long as the chickens don't poop in here," Abbie said, gazing at Lachie's workmanship. "It's incredible."

He moved closer to her. "We just need to get some furniture. Maybe a little kitchen so she can pretend to cook."

"Oh, and are you going to have tea parties together?" She threw him a smile.

"Of course. Isn't that what daddies do with their daughters?" he said, his heart swelling. He would happily have tea parties with Hannah and let her paint his face with makeup if that was what she wanted. Hannah would get all the attention she needed and then some. He loved playing with her and spending time with her. It didn't matter what they did.

CHAPTER 21

The city wasn't so bad, Lachie thought, as they strode down the busy, wide lane of Queen Street. Everyone he passed had their heads down, focused on where they were going and what needed to be done. In the country, people had time to stop and chat. Everyone knew everyone.

Townsville hadn't been this busy. The northern Queensland town had always struck him as being just big enough for some night life and a change of scenery. But the towering concrete buildings and traffic noise of Brisbane was something else. He supposed he could see the appeal in a short visit, but he knew he couldn't live here. The pollution and noise was enough to send him running. Give him the outback any day.

He glanced sideways at Abbie and wondered if she thought the same. Her body was tense, and she gripped Hannah's hand tightly. Was she scared she'd lose Hannah if she let go? It was certainly possible.

"Here it is." Abbie pointed to the restaurant where they were meeting her parents.

They walked inside and after giving her name, they were shown to their seats on the balcony.

"Wine list." The waiter passed the leather-bound folder to Lachie.

Abbie reached over and pushed the menu back at the server. "No alcohol thanks. Just water."

Lachie threw her an appreciative glance. She looked good all made up. Her swept-up hair exposed the elegant line of her neck and called for him to explore its smooth contours. And as for her mouth, the pinkish hue high-lighted the full sweep of her lips and reminded him of all the talented things she could do with them.

"Can we go to Australia Zoo?" Hannah asked as they chatted about all the touristy things they could do during their short city visit.

Abbie pushed a strand of her daughter's hair behind her ear. "That's on the Sunshine Coast, and we only have a few days. Why don't we go to the museum and see the dinosaurs?"

Hannah shrugged. "Dad said he'd take me to Winton to see the dinosaur trail."

Lachie grinned. "It's actually very good. They found real fossils out there."

"Besides," Hannah continued, "he's the one who's never been here before. What do you want to do?" She looked up at him with shinning blue eyes, the exact same as his own.

Lachie leaned back and scratched his cheek. "I would like to go to a movie. Haven't done that in years."

"Yes." Hannah squealed. "Which one? There's a new Disney movie I really want to see."

He looked to Abbie, who smiled and nodded.

"Sure, squirt." He leaned in close. "Do they still sell popcorn in cinemas? The really buttery, salty stuff?"

She nodded enthusiastically. "You can get lots of flavours now. I like caramel."

"There are your grandparents," Abbie said as Adam and Judith approached. After hugs were exchanged, they sat down and turned to Lachie.

"It's so nice to see you again. How are you enjoying the city?" Judith asked.

Lachie smiled back. "It's great. I can see why you like it."

"Oh, we don't come into the city very often. We have a house by the river, which is nice and peaceful. You really should be staying with us." Judith turned to her daughter.

"No, Mum. I told you, we wanted to stay in the city so we were close to everything."

"Okay." She exhaled. "Do come for dinner one night though."

"We'll see." Abbie faced Lachie and rolled her eyes so only he could see. Abbie had told him all about her parents and their plans for her and Hannah. He liked them as well as he could after their brief encounters but believed whatever Abbie said about them. He hoped they liked him and would continue to support their relationship. That was the whole reason for this trip, after all.

"So why the trip out anyway?" Judith asked.

Abbie shuffled in her seat. "We have some news. I'm

sorry I didn't tell you before, but Lachie is Hannah's biological father."

Her parents' mouths dropped so low they almost hit the floor.

"What?" Judith said. "Is that why you went out there?"

"No." Abbie gestured to her daughter. "I'll tell you all the details later. We just wanted to tell you in person that Lachie's her dad and that we're dating."

After a short pause, Judith turned to Lachie. "Congratulations. It must have come as a bit of a shock."

"Yeah, it did. A good one though." He put his arm around Hannah's shoulder, and she snuggled in for a hug. "I couldn't be happier."

Adam chuckled his deep, hearty laugh. "So the mystery is finally solved."

"I'm so glad it's him." Judith patted her daughter's arm, and Lachie noted the look of understanding that passed between them.

"Me too," said Abbie, and she turned to meet his gaze.

"Me three," said Hannah, with the biggest smile stretching across her pixie face.

～

As hard as she now looked, Abbie couldn't see the appeal of the city anymore. Once this was the only world she'd wanted to belong in, and now she found it somehow lacking. Being back in the city hadn't made her wish she still lived within its sophisticated embrace. All it had done was reinforce that she'd changed and now wanted different things. She liked being in the country where it was warm and welcoming, and replete with community spirit. That was the life she wanted for her daughter and the life she wanted for herself.

That night, in the peaceful confines of their hotel apartment, after Hannah was sound asleep in her bed, Lachie pulled Abbie into his arms. His hands framed her face and his mouth found hers. Her lips parted, her hands gripped the back of his neck, and then there was nothing but urgency, heat, and need between them. She entwined her hands around his nape and moulded herself against him. In Lachie's arms was where she belonged now.

When he ran his palm up and along her delicate spine, she shivered. Her own hands snuck beneath his shirt, and he couldn't contain his groan as her fingertips trailed across his hip and stomach.

"God, I'll never get enough of you," he said, his hands tangling in her hair as she pressed herself against him and her mouth met his.

Her fingers flicked down his shirt buttons and when she pushed the cotton off his shoulders, he had all the answers he'd need. She had no intention of stopping.

He lifted her into his arms and carried her to the bed. As he laid her down, their gazes met. She'd never seen his eyes look a more brilliant blue or appear so luminous. She kissed him again and lost herself in the beauty and warmth of the only man she'd ever want.

CHAPTER 22

A few weeks after returning from the city, Abbie found herself being blindfolded. She squeezed her daughter's hand, the other one groping around in the dark. "Don't let me trip over."

"It's not far," Hannah assured her as they walked further away from the house.

"Why do I need a blindfold?" Abbie raised her hand to remove the fabric from her eyes.

"Mum, it's a surprise. Don't ruin it." Hannah's insistence had Abbie dropping her hand to follow blindly.

Unable to see, her other senses were working overtime. Spring was a spectacular time in the outback. The temperature was rising, and Harriet's garden was blooming with bright colours and fragrant smells. She could smell perfume from the flowers mix with the earthy country air.

Finally, Hannah stopped her, and Abbie stood awkwardly for a moment. "What's going on?"

Then she felt Lachie's heat and smell in front of her. She would know that scent anywhere.

He stepped forward, cupped the back of her head, and kissed her. Her response was instant. She fitted herself against him and wound her arms around his neck. Never would she get enough of his kisses, of his love.

His mouth left hers to trail sweet kisses down her throat. She moaned and groped at his hair, loving the thickness of it in her fingers.

Then, Lachie released the knot of the blindfold and she blinked open her eyes.

Sitting on the grass in front of her was a table and two wooden chairs. It was decorated with a white cloth and covered with flowers, twinkling fairy lights, and all her favourite foods. Crackers and round white cheeses, dried apricots, almonds, olives, and bread sticks all lay temptingly arranged.

"What's all this?" She stepped forward to better enjoy the delicacies in front of her.

"Happy birthday, Abbie." Lachie stood behind her and wrapped his arms around her waist, snuggling into her neck.

Abbie stroked his arms contentedly.

"Do you like it? I helped," Hannah said, skipping around the table in her best pink and white dress.

"It's beautiful. What did I do to deserve this? To deserve both of you?"

Lachie unravelled himself from her, and she took in his clean-shaven appearance. His crisp white shirt looked new, and instead of jeans he wore black trousers, which looked freshly ironed. She hadn't even known Brigadier Station had an iron.

Lachie leaned down and said something to Hannah before they both turned conspiratorially to Abbie.

Then Lachie reached out and took one of her hands. Hannah took her other.

"Abigail Forsyth, you are the woman of my dreams, the mother of my child." His voice was choked with emotion, and she watched him struggle to keep it in check, all the while her own heart thumped loudly.

Then he sank onto one knee and looked up at her. "I love you. You have no idea how much. I never want to be anywhere but with you and Hannah."

Hannah placed her spare hand on his shoulder and looked up at her. "Will you marry my daddy?"

Abbie couldn't speak. Tears trickled down her cheeks. She was overcome by emotion.

Lachie put out his hand and presented her with a simple silver ring with a small, shining diamond. "Abbie? Will you be my wife?"

She nodded through her tears and went to them, hugging them together and kissing both their cheeks. Hannah squirmed away and started chanting, "She said yes, she said yes."

Abbie laughed, then turned serious eyes back to Lachie. "Are you sure?"

"Are you?"

"Yes. I am. I love you."

They rose together, their mouths tightly pressed.

Abbie knew in her heart that they brought out the best

in one another and would always be there to support and comfort each other.

She was in love and optimistic for their future. They would make a life out here, together.

Brigadier Station was where they belonged, now and forever.

CHAPTER 23

*L*achie sat alone on the verandah. The sun was setting over the flat horizon. He could see Abbie playing with Hannah in the front paddock.

Her blonde hair was pulled back into a ponytail to reveal the smooth pale skin of her nape. He'd memorised every delicate contour and satin-soft curve of her body. He knew he would love her deeply until the day he died.

Meghan, Darcy, and Harriet's voices floated on the breeze as they came outside to join him. They were spending the weekend at Brigadier Station so Darcy could view a horse he was considering buying and adding to his stud.

Harriet handed Lachie a frosty can of Coke before sitting next to him. He turned to his brother, who seemed brighter than usual. Like a heavy fog had lifted.

Meghan was staring out at the sunset. She had always loved the colours of the country, and time and hardships hadn't changed that.

Lachie was so thankful to her for walking out on their

wedding day. She had found true love and happiness with Darcy, and he had found everything he could ever want with Abbie. He'd never known such joy or that sharing his life with someone could feel so complete and so right.

"They've fit right in, haven't they?" Darcy nodded in Abbie and Hannah's direction. Hannah was kicking a ball to her mother, creating mini dust storms in her wake.

"They sure have." Lachie smiled. "Abbie's going part-time at the hospital next year so she can teach Hannah through School of the Air."

"She won't miss working? I thought she loved it," Meghan said.

"She'll still do two or three shifts a week," Lachie replied. "But Hannah is growing up so quickly and she wants to spend more time with her. We both do."

Darcy sipped his drink. A can of Coke, Lachie noted, and Meghan was drinking plain water. "School of the Air will be a big change after state school."

Harriet leaned forward. "Hannah wants to be just like her dad. She said that if it was good enough for him, it's good enough for her. Paige has offered to help out, and they're planning lots of activities and meet-ups next year."

The group watched as Abbie and Hannah finished their game and walked up to join them.

"Uncle Darcy, will you teach me how to campdraft?" Hannah asked.

Darcy smiled at her. "Sure, if your parents say it's okay."

Hannah turned her most angelic face to Lachie, and his heart melted. "You'd need a good horse for that," he said.

From the corner of his eye, he saw Darcy take Meghan's hand and exchange a knowing look.

"Actually, Hannah, I was wondering if you'd look after Molly for me for a while," Meghan said referring to her old but loyal horse.

Hannah squealed with delight, while all the adults turned curious eyes on Meghan.

"What? You love that horse," Lachie said.

"I do. The thing is, I'm not allowed to ride for the next few months." A wide grin spread across her mouth.

Harriet jumped to her feet, spilling her drink in her wake. "Are you pregnant?"

Meghan nodded. "Three months along, and everything is completely normal and healthy."

Harriet and Abbie rushed over with hugs and congratulations.

Lachie pulled his brother close for a man-hug. "I'm so happy for you. I know how much you and Meghan wanted this."

Darcy looked at his wife, the love in his eyes obvious and strong. "We're so happy. I can't say I'm not scared though. Losing the last one was hard on both of us. I don't know if we could go through that again."

Lachie's heart ached for his brother. He couldn't imagine losing Hannah. "I'm sure everything will be fine, and in a few months, you'll be changing nappies and complaining about sleepless nights."

Darcy laughed. "I can't wait."

They looked over to see Hannah place her ear against Meghan's still-flat stomach. "Hi baby. I'm your cousin, Hannah. I can't wait to meet you," she said to the belly.

"You might need to give her a sibling one of these days," Darcy said.

"Abbie and I have already talked about it. After the wedding, we'll start trying."

"How great will that be?" Darcy said. "To have our kids grow up together and spend their holidays here on Brigadier Station?"

"It sure will be," Lachie agreed, remembering all the good times he and his brothers had spent together at the very same place.

Harriet joined her sons. "Gosh, I'm so happy." She hugged Darcy for a long time and when she withdrew, there were tears in her eyes. "Children are such gifts. More than that, really. They're our legacies."

She pulled both her sons together and put her arms around each of their waists. "Abbie and I would like everyone to come here for Christmas this year. I've already asked Noah, and he's agreed."

"It will be Hannah's first outback Christmas," Lachie said, watching his daughter. She proudly wore blue jeans and a pink cowgirl shirt. Just to add flare to the outfit, she also wore a sparkly tiara. *That's my girl*, he thought. His little princess.

He couldn't wait for Christmas. He would get to play Santa and spoil her. He would make up for all the Christmases they had missed spending together. "Sounds like a great idea, Mum."

Darcy nodded in agreement. "Christmas at Brigadier Station. I'm sure it will be an event we'll never forget."

The Brothers of Brigadier Station

(#1 in the Brigadier Station series)

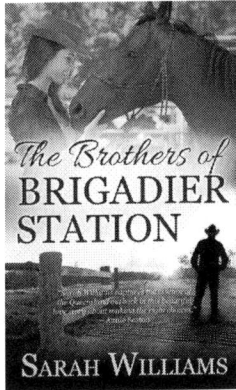

*She came to the outback to marry the love of her life. She just didn't
expect him to be her fiancé's younger brother.*

When Meghan Flanagan, a vet-nurse from Townsville, moves to
Brigadier Station in outback Queensland to marry the man of
her dreams, she is shocked to discover that perhaps her fiancé
isn't the man she wants waiting for her at the altar. The man
she's destined to marry, just might be his younger brother.

Cautious of women after a disastrous past relationship, Darcy is
happy living on his beloved cattle station, spending his spare
time riding horses, going to rodeos and campdrafting. He didn't
expect the perfect woman show up on his doorstep. Engaged to
his brother.

With the wedding only hours away, Meghan must make the
decision of a lifetime. But, her betrayal could tear the family
apart. She knows all too well the pain of losing loved ones and
being alone.

Now that she has the family she so desperately wants; will she risk losing it all?

Buy The Brothers of Brigadier Station

The Sky over Brigadier Station

(#2 in the Brigadier Station series)

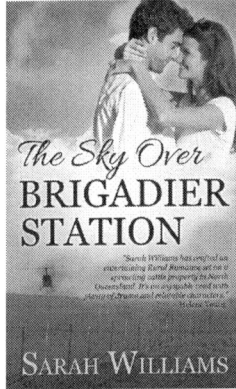

He guards his heart. She yields to no man. Will a chance encounter set a course for true love?

Noah McGuire buries his demons deep inside. But when he's forced to return home to Brigadier Station to collect his inheritance, he can no longer avoid digging up his painful past. With the wounds of childhood trauma reopened, his world plunges into darkness until a beautiful pilot sets his heart afire.

Riley Sinclair isn't afraid to fly against the wind. While the spunky helicopter pilot's cattle herding business ruffles the feathers of most men, the handsome Noah seems different. But as demand for her skills grows, she worries that giving into passion could keep her dreams grounded.

As their chemistry soars, an unexpected tragedy throws their lives and their budding romance into a tailspin.

Can Noah and Riley leave their baggage behind to let love fly free?

The Sky over Brigadier Station is the second standalone book in the captivating Brigadier Station Western romance series. If you like flawed characters, simmering scenes, and stunning Australian and New Zealand settings, then you'll love Sarah Williams' rugged tale.

Buy The Sky over Brigadier Station

The Legacies of Brigadier Station

(#3 in the Brigadier Station series)

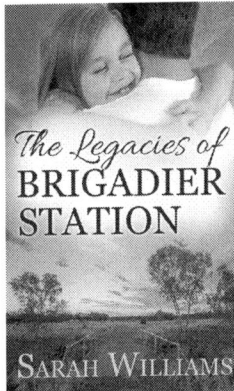

Can Lachie be the father Hannah needs? And the man Abbie deserves?

Lachie McGuire is trying to make a fresh start. He's sobered up and is making amends for all the people he has hurt and the pain he has caused. But some of his past actions have consequences. Even if he doesn't remember them.

Needing her independence, single-mum Abbie Forsyth accepted a nursing position in the small outback town of Julia Creek and uprooted her daughter, Hannah from the only life she had ever known. Now, in the dusty, sun burned land they are creating a life together, just the two of them.

When Lachie is injured and needs medical assistance, Abbie is there for him. She's by his side every step of the way, including letting him stay with them while he recovers from surgery. But Abbie knows how volatile life with an addict can be and she has to think about her daughter's safety above her own growing affection for the handsome grazier.

Then tragedy strikes the small rural town and secrets begin to unravel…

Return to the Outback for the third instalment in the bestselling Brigadier Station series.

Buy The Legacies of Brigadier Station

The Outback Governess

A Sweet Outback Novella

(#4 in the Brigadier Station series)

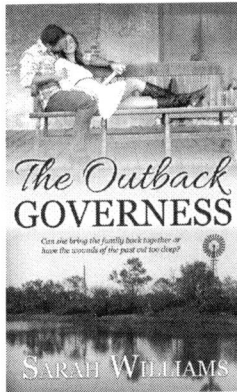

Can Paige bring the family back together or have the wounds of the past cut too deep?

When special-needs teacher Paige, takes up the position of Governess for three young children in the Queensland outback, she has no idea just how much and how quickly she would come to love the dusty, dry country, and the family who desperately need her.

Logan was heartbroken when his wife died, leaving him to raise their three children with the help of his aging parents on their remote cattle station. To avoid the constant reminder of the love he lost, he works on a mine in Mt Isa, meaning he only sees his family week on, week off.

But then tragedy strikes and Paige and Logan are forced to work together to look after the children, alone on the station. As well as being their teacher, Paige also becomes a substitute mother and teaches Logan how to be a parent again. A role he has avoided since losing his wife.

If you enjoyed The Brigadier Station series then you will love learning about distance education and how thousands of rural children are educated with the help of their parents and governesses.

The Outback Governess is a sweet, clean western romance by bestselling Australian author, Sarah Williams.

Buy The Outback Governess

The Dairy Farmer's Daughter

(#1 in the Heart of the Hinterland series)

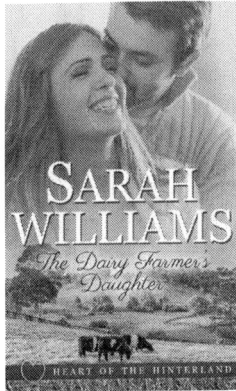

Will Justin choose riches over his heritage or will he find a love more valuable than all the money in the world?

Justin would have preferred to stay in the city and pretend it was an ordinary day. A day that didn't include a funeral for a father he'd barely known...

Justin Wheeler is not a country boy. He could have been, if his mother had stayed married to his father and not moved back to the city when he was only a toddler. But now that his estranged father is dead and he has inherited the dairy farm, Justin finds himself considering if the life he is living is actually the life he wants.

Family means everything to Freya Montgomery. She loves living on the land and helping to grow the family business. She knows how important agriculture is to their small hinterland community, so when Justin arrives in town and is offered a generous price from a housing developer to buy his property, Freya must convince him not to accept the deal and instead lease the land to her family.

The Dairy Farmer's Daughter is the first novella in an exciting new sexy, small-town series called "Heart of the Hinterland" by Bestselling author, Sarah Williams.

Buy The Dairy Farmer's Daughter

ABOUT THE AUTHOR

Bestselling author Sarah Williams spent her childhood chasing sheep, riding horses and picking Kiwi fruit on the family orchard in rural New Zealand. After a decade travelling, Sarah moved to Queensland to enjoy the endless summer, pristine beaches and tropical rainforests.

When she's not absorbed in her fictional writing world, Sarah is running after her family of four kids, one husband, two dogs, a horse and a cat.

She is Founder and CEO of Serenade Publishing, hosts the weekly podcast/vlog *Write with Love*, runs writers workshops and retreats, mentors and supports her peers to achieve their publishing dreams.

Sarah is regularly checking social media when she really should be cleaning.

To receive updates and free books, sign up for her mailing list.

www.sarahwilliamsauthor.com

f facebook.com/sarahwilliamswriter

⊙ instagram.com/sarahwilliamsauthor

BB bookbub.com/profile/sarah-williams

g goodreads.com/goodreadscomsarahwilliams

ACKNOWLEDGMENTS

My sincere thanks to all my writer friends who support and encourage me on this amazing journey. They include but are not limited to Kelly Ethan, Michelle Dalton and my incredible editor Lauren Clark.

To Myles Pollard for his amazing performance in the audiobooks.

As always, a big thank you and much love to my family for all your support and for putting up with me while I write. I love you all.

And to you, dear reader. Thank you for choosing this book to read. I know there are many other distractions and entertainment options available these days, so thank you for joining Lachie, Abbie, Hannah and me on this journey.

48735877R00129

Printed in Poland
by Amazon Fulfillment
Poland Sp. z o.o., Wrocław